Rosanada Requiem

Josué Raúl Conte

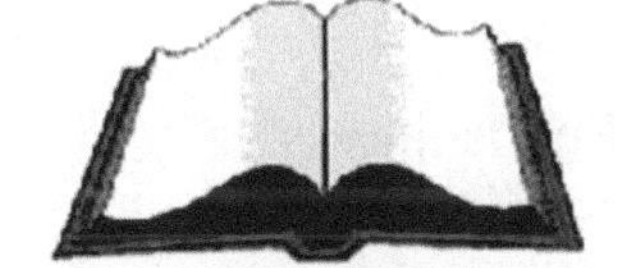

CCB Publishing
British Columbia, Canada

Rosanada Requiem: Volume 3 of the Rosanada Trilogy

ISBN-13 978-1-926585-34-5
Second Edition

Library and Archives Canada Cataloguing in Publication
Conte, Josué Raúl, 1969-
Rosanada Requiem / written by Josué Raúl Conte. – 2nd ed.
(The Rosanada trilogy ; v. 3)
ISBN 978-1-926585-34-5
I. Title. II. Series:°Conte, Josué Raúl, 1969- . Rosanada trilogy.
PS3603.O5624R67 2009 813'.6 C2009-904118-9

Publisher: CCB Publishing
British Columbia, Canada
www.ccbpublishing.com

Volume 3 of

The Rosanada Trilogy

1

Malleus Shamrock

It was a dark dismal night with occasional bursts of jagged lightening piercing the heavens. Glad that he did not have to go out into the approaching storm, Malleus Shamrock entered the living room of the rectory of Santiago Church searching for his breviary. It was already ten thirty and he had to finish his prayers before midnight. Although he was sure he had left it on the bookcase by the large casement window, it was nowhere to be seen.

"Excuse me Father Julian," he said, addressing his young vicar who was engrossed in reading the *Rosanada News* and appeared not to notice that he had entered the room. "Have you seen my breviary lying around here somewhere?" "No, sorry, I haven't, Father Mel." the vicar mumbled without taking his eyes from his newspaper. "Perhaps Monsignor has seen it." He was speaking of Monsignor Pierre Petit, a retired priest who lived at Santiago parish and helped out wherever he was needed and who was watching the evening news on television, while sipping a glass of Port, for, he always insisted, medicinal purposes. As a missionary in Morocco, he had developed leptospirosis and had come to Rosanada to receive treatment for the symptoms of the disease. He then settled down in the archdiocese as pastor of St. Cassiel's Church, when Father Billie J. King was removed and defrocked as a result of his part in the Halloween fiasco a few years back, until he retired and moved into the rectory at Santiago where he helped the pastor in any way that he could.

"*Oui, d'accord*, I did see it," the monsignor replied with a decidedly French accent which was to be expected since he was from Paris where he attended La Sorbonne and the seminary of St. Sulpice. "You left it in the sacristy on the counter, right below where we keep the chalices, ciboriums and the communion wine and wafers. I saw it when I had the seven o'clock Mass this evening."

"Of course." Mel replied with a sigh of relief. "I remember now. I had it there this morning when I said Mass. I'll run over and get it. If anyone calls, I'll be right back."

Fr. Julian resumed reading the *News* and Monsignor Petit returned to his television, both expecting the evening to be like every other in the rectory. Soon events would take a bizarre, unexpected, and frightening turn.

After picking up his top coat and an umbrella in the closet by the entrance door of the rectory, he ventured out into the night. The wind was beginning to blow and howl through the tall oak tress that lined the walkway from the rectory to the church. Santiago parish was located in a very poor neighborhood but Marco Lamadrid, the pastor who built the church years ago, had the foresight to build a tall and sturdy iron fence around the entire property. As he approached the church, he was startled by the appearance of someone walking around the side of the building. It was a man with a cap pulled down over his eyes who shuffled slowly toward him.

"Evening, Father Shamrock," the man called out.

Mel was relieved to recognize the voice of the security guard he had hired to patrol the premises.

"Good evening, Valin," he responded. Shamrock had given Valin Vogel a job out of the goodness of his heart. The man was down and out, in his sixties, rather eccentric, and had not been able to find work to support himself.

As Valin continued walking in the direction of the convent that stood behind the church, Mel pulled his keys from his pocket and unlocked the main door of Santiago. He often came to the church at night to sit in the darkness and watch the flickering votive candles on the candle rack along the side wall. Slowly he made his way passed the statue of Santiago—St. James—and went to kneel before the very modern tabernacle. The red glass sanctuary lamp on the wall above the Reserved Eucharist flickered with candle light radiating mystery into the darkness of the church, casting shadows that created strange shapes swirling and hovering around him. He loved to come to the church at night and be alone with the mystery of God and His Presence. However, it was getting late and he had to finish saying his breviary, so he got up from kneeling there in the dark and went into the sacristy, turning on the light switch as he entered the room. Unprepared for what he saw, he froze in his tracks. Sprawled on the floor in a pool of blood was Sister Megan McGrath, a young nun who was one of the teachers in Santiago Elementary School. A knife was protruding from her body and a strange pole that was decorated with colorful red streamers and bright red beads was piercing her heart, pinning her to the floor. A petite young woman, she was wearing a white, ruffled peasant blouse and a bright green full skirt that was pushed up to her waist, revealing her black lace panties. The knife, a curious looking blade with an elaborate black ebony handle, was plunged up to its hilt in her lower abdomen where blood was still oozing from the wound it made. Although horrified by what he saw, he managed to walk around the body and pick up the phone that sat on the counter where the altar linens were kept. Quickly he punched in 911. To the voice that answered, he responded as calmly as he could: "Get me the police."

Within moments, Malleus heard a rather metallic sounding voice, say, "Chief Detective Callahan speaking."

"There has been a homicide at Santiago Church in the Gas'du Hills. In the sacristy... please come at once."

"We are on our way. Don't touch anything and keep people away from the crime scene," Callahan snapped brusquely.

As he waited for the police to arrive, Mel got a tall drinking glass from the sacristy WC and poured it half full with sacramental wine and sipped it slowly to calm his nerves.

Within minutes, the police arrived and began photographing Sister's Megan's mutilated body. The detective assigned to the case introduced himself as Ariel Zadek and his colleague that was with him as the coroner.

"Are you the one who discovered the corpse?" Zadek asked as he bent over to get a closer look at the body.

"Yes, I discovered her just before I phoned. I'd say it was about 10:45 this evening."

Mel watched as Detective Zadek drew a chalk diagram around the body, as it lay on the oak floor of the sacristy. When the coroner gave him the sign to continue, he then directed the forensics crew to recover the knife and the strange pole that pierced the woman's heart, after securing finger prints from them both. Quickly they zipped the body of Sister Megan into a body bag, put it on a gurney, and wheeled it out to their van that was parked at the door of the sacristy with the coroner accompanying the body.

"Who else is on the premises tonight?" Detective Zadek inquired.

Shamrock judged that the detective was Jewish, about thirty years of age, and in a hurry to get to the facts of the case.

"Quite a few people, Detective. There is Monsignor Petit, a retired pastor who lives here, and Fr. Julian, my vicar, and thirteen nuns in the convent behind the church. For security we also have a man who roams the grounds, Valin Vogel. who has an apartment on the third floor of the rectory and works as a handy man and takes care of the furnace.

"I will question everyone. Also I also need some background information on the murdered woman. What can you tell me about her?"

"I will be glad to give you all the information I can. Shall we go to the rectory where we can talk and you can interview the other priests? Then I will take you to the convent and introduced you to Sister Shiela. She is the convent coordinator and can give you much more information than I can about Sister Megan, the murdered woman."

"You say she was a sister?" Zadek asked skeptically. "You mean she was a nun? I mean she wasn't dressed like a nun. I'm not Catholic, I'm Jewish, but I thought nuns wore black dresses and veils." Zadek looked to Mel for some answers.

"Detective, many things have changed. The past few years have caused a lot of turmoil within the Church. Many nuns wear whatever they want to and usually do."

A loud rumble of thunder and a flash of lightning that struck near the church, heralding a violent burst of driving rain, sent Father Mel looking for a flashlight in a cabinet in the sacristy. With flashlight in hand, he opened a door in one side of the room, revealing a flight of stairs leading down to the lower level of the church into the underground passage way that went to the rectory.

Motioning for Detective Zadek to follow him, he explained: "When Father Lamadrid built the church, he had underground passageways made from the church to the rectory, the parish hall, and to the convent to facilitate the state of the art central heating and cooling system that we have here at Santiago. When the weather is bad, as it is right now in this thunderstorm or when there is a blizzard, we priests often go from one building to the other using the underground passageways. Most people are not aware that they exist and they are off limits to all but the clergy and Valin Vogel, our security guard."

Quickly walking through the dark, dimly lit cement block tunnel, they reached the rectory, and after climbing a flight of stairs with Detective Zadek right behind him, Father Mel pulled the keys from his pocket and opened the door into a large pantry just off the kitchen. Monsignor Petit and Father Julian were still in the living room when they entered. "Excuse me," Mel said softy, "this is Detective Zadek. He wants to ask each of you a few questions. A crime has been committed…"

Turning off the fifty-two inch television that Mel had bought to watch NFL football, Monsignor Petit, squinting his eyes, asked intently, "What happened?"

Laying aside the book he was reading, Father Julian sat up, abandoning his prone position on the sofa, and waited attentively for Mel to explain.

"When I went to get my breviary…"

Abruptly Detective Zadek interrupted him. "A girl was murdered in your church."

Fright, horror, and unbelief were written on the faces of the two priests.

"It is Sister Megan," Father Mel explained, overcome with emotion. "Someone killed Sister Megan McGrath in the sacristy." His hand trembled as he set the flashlight down on the table by the sofa.

"Where were you, Reverend, earlier this evening? We are setting the time of death at about two or three hours ago judging from the physical evidence."

"I was in my room," Mel answered. "Upstairs."

"And you other two?" Zadek asked, glancing first at Monsignor Petit and then at Father Julian.

"*Eh bien.* When my Mass was over at about eight this evening, I went to the Parish Hall for a meeting and was there until about ten. Then I was here watching the news on television," Monsignor Petit spoke softly, but with precision. He was a tall, thin man and the skin on his face was taut, revealing the bone structure underneath. The veins on the backs of his hands were bluish as they often are on the hands of older people. Although it was late at night, he was impeccably dressed in black trousers and a black clerical shirt.

"And I," answered Father Julian, "I went to see a movie and got home shortly after ten." Much younger than Monsignor Petit, he was wearing a gray Notre Dame sweatshirt and gray slacks.

"I will have more questions for all of you later, but right now I would like to know more about the murdered girl. Father Shamrock, what can you tell me about her?"

"Not much really. She was about twenty-four, She tried very hard to please people. She was teaching second grade in our school. I did not know her very well. She just came here for the first time a few months ago," Mel answered softly and then added, "I am sure Sister Shiela will be able to give you more information than I can. She would know about the Ardorines that she is in charge of.

"Ardorines?" Zadek asked.

"Yes, the name of their congregation is the Daughters of the Holy Ardor—so they are called Ardorines. Their headquarters is in Rome. I will take you over to the convent and introduce you to Sister Shiela, the superior—I mean, coordinator."

"That is all right, Reverend," Zadek replied, glancing out at the casement windows. "The storm seems to be slacking up now. If you don't mind, I will go there by myself. Just show me where it is, please."

Mel accompanied Detective Zadek to the front door of the rectory and pointed out to him the direction to take to the convent. The rain had stopped, but the wind was still howling in the oak trees and blowing withered leaves across the front lawn. The image of the dead girl haunted Mel as he closed the door behind the detective and retired to his room. He knew what he had to do. He had to phone Bishop Renato Del'Ano, the vicar general, and tell him about the horrible events at Santiago. Although he dreaded calling the VG, he went right to the phone and dialed his number at Casa St. Popola's.

"Del'Ano here," the voice on the other end of the line said forcefully with a no-nonsense sound about it.

"Your Excellency, this is Malleus Shamrock at Santiago Church." He decided to come right to the point. "One of the nuns was murdered tonight in the sacristy of the church."

"Oh my God! That is all we need now! Call the proper authorities and keep me informed," Bishop Del'Ano said crisply and hung up before Malleus could say another word.

Although he tried to sleep, he could not because of thoughts of the dead Megan that haunted him. When he finally fell asleep, he was caught up in a terrifying dream of his mother lying bleeding in an open coffin before the altar in the church.

2

Sister Shiela

Who could that be ringing the door chimes at this time of night in this miserable weather? Sister Shiela closed the book she was reading, left her room, and started down the stairs to answer the door. Since she never went to bed before midnight, she was fully dressed in a dark green tailored suit and a white silk tailored shirt. She glanced in the mirror on the wall near the door to see if her coiffure was still all in place. After arranging a couple of loose strands of her hennaed hair, she snapped on the porch light and, glancing out the pane of glass in the upper part of the door, saw a rather strange looking man who was holding his police badge out for her to see.

Opening the door a few inches—it had a chain guard in place, she called to him, "What can I do for you, Officer?" Before he could answer, she snapped: "Hand me your badge; I want to inspect it." She was not about to be taken in by any imposters who thought they could force their way into the convent with a fake badge.

"Yes, Ma'am." He slipped the badge in through the door that was open about four inches. "I am Detective Zadek from homicide. A woman has been murdered in the church. I believe she was one of your nuns."

"How horrible!" she exclaimed, as she felt the blood

drain from her face. "It must be Sister Megan. I wondered where she was. She went to the church about eight this evening and has not yet returned.

"She won't be coming back, Ma'am. We took her body away a short time ago. I would like to know more about her. What can you tell me?"

Shiela put the chain guard back in its place and opened the door. "Come in, Officer." She led him into the very modern living room of the convent that was tastefully furnished with Scandinavian appointments. A roaring fire was blazing in the stone fireplace, as a large oak log crackled and sizzled. Taking a seat on the black leather sofa in front of the fireplace, Sister Shiela motioned for him to be seated. He settled in a Barcelona chair near her.

"What is your full name, please," Zadek asked as he opened a notepad and began to write.

"Shiela Cromlech Dolman."

"Thank you, Ma'am. Now what can you tell me about Sister Megan?" he inquired. "How long have you known her?"

"I have known her about 3 or 4 years. She got a scholarship to Madonna High School in Derryville where I was the principal. Good student. When she finished high school, she entered our novitiate." Sister Shiela noticed that her manicure needed attention. One of her nails had become chipped and needed to be touched up with her Red Dragon nail polish.

"Tell me about her family background." As he appeared to be sizing her up, Detective Zadek was carefully making notes of all she said.

"Well, she was orphaned at an early age. She was about two when her parents were both killed in a car crash. The courts put her with black foster parents who always had eight or ten foster children in their care. Consequently, she did not get much attention in that home, and I think that is why she always seemed to be hungry for affection, trying very hard to win approval from everyone." Shiela sighed and thought a few moments before continuing. "She was shy and retiring, when we first got to know her, but she has blossomed, since becoming an Ardorine."

A sudden flash of lightening and a loud clap of thunder made Shiela apprehensive. As far back as she could remember, she had always hated electrical storms.

"Can you think of anyone who would want to kill her?" As she talked, Zadek was scribbling rapidly on a pad jotting down everything she said.

"Absolutely not," Sister Shiela replied. "Will you return her body to us here in the convent? We will want to have her funeral here at Santiago, of course." Shiela thought of all the things that would have to be done to get ready for the burial.

"Yes, Ma'am, I will see to that myself," Zadek replied, and then asked: "Would you mind telling me what Sister Megan was doing in the church this evening?" He pulled a pack of cigarettes from his pocket. "Mind if I smoke?"

"Not at all to both questions. Sister Megan went over there to arrange for a special liturgy that we were planning for the women of the parish." Shiela toyed with a ballpoint pen that she picked up from the cocktail table that sat in front of the sofa.

"When we found her she had some kind of pole trimmed with red streamers and red beads plunged through her heart, and there was a knife with an ebony handle stuck in her lower abdomen. Any idea where the pole and the knife might have come from?"

"They sound like things we use in our liturgies."

"Just what are liturgies—you mean the Mass?"

"No, I am talking about prayers and rituals that put us in touch with ourselves and creation. Because the Church's liturgies are so boring, we have implemented them with some of our own." Shiela patted her reddish hair with her hand and pulled a handkerchief from her jacket pocket and daubed her eyes with it, being careful not to smudge her eye makeup. "I just can't believe she is dead," she said sadly, more to herself than to Zadek. Then wiping away a tear, she added: "I just want you to know, Detective, that if there is anything I can do to help find her killer— anything at all, just let me know."

"Well, I have one more question I need to ask you now."

"Anything," she replied, tucking her handkerchief into the pocket of her suit.

"Where were the knife and the staff with the red streamers kept?"

"They were in a closet in the sacristy. We were planning to use them next week at a special gathering in the church for the women." She rose to her feet to terminate the interview. It was late and she, as principal of the entire twelve grades, had to be in her office in the school early in the morning.

"Well," said Zadek rising to his feet. "I will have to

seal off the room of the murdered woman. No one is to enter it, until I can get a search warrant to examine the contents. If you would kindly direct me to her room, I will seal the door."

"Of course, follow me." Shiela led him up the stairs to Megan's room. "You can seal the door, but you cannot search the room until you have the warrant."

When Megan's room was secured to his satisfaction as a crime scene, Zadek eyed Shiela carefully and said: "That is all for now, but I assure you, I will be back to question you and all the nuns further. And when I return, I will have a search warrant."

After escorting the detective out of the convent, Sister Shiela went into the nun's chapel in the east wing. Because it was now past midnight, all the other sisters had retired for the night and the chapel was deserted. A flickering flame burned under the large bronze laver that stood on the floor in the center of the chapel and was surrounded by two rows of cushions where the nuns had sat earlier in the evening for their night prayers together. Picking up a few grains of incense from the floor beside the laver, Shiela sprinkled them on the fire. Soon the fragrance of jasmine incense filled the room. In silent meditation, Shiela gazed up at the gigantic painting of the Goddess Ix Chel that reached from floor to ceiling on the wall behind the altar. She herself had painted the icon of the Moon Goddess, the Lady Rainbow—her very own special guide, standing totally nude behind a waterfall that obscured her radiant sexuality and cascaded into a large pool filled with water lilies that surrounded the altar, except for the large stones the priestess stood on to work her spells. In her hand Ix Chel was holding a great snake that appeared to twist and turn, writhing to be set free. It amused Shiela when unsuspecting priests, laywomen of the parish, and children from the school saw the painting of IX Chel and thought that it was a very beautiful and special painting of the Virgin Mary.

As she drifted into a reverie remembering her dedication to the Goddess. Shiela's eyes fastened on Ix Chel's face. It was only five years since that she had flown down to Cozumel and stayed at the woman's retreat house on the very spot where Ix Chel had been venerated for centuries. Extremely discouraged with her life, because of the anti-feminism she had encountered in the Church, she was considering dropping out of the Ardorines, when she arrived in Mexico. Utterly distraught and fed up with the phallocratic patriarchal establishment, her life as a nun had withered into nothingness. She was a nun—spelled none. Because she was a woman, she was a second class citizen in the Church. So that she would be well-educated, they sent her to the state university, where she had learned that women are considered inferior, according to the theologians down through the centuries.

Fortunately Hilda, the mother provincial, had suggested that she go down to one of the women's retreat houses on the Island of Cozumel in the brilliant cerulean waters of the Caribbean just off the Yucatan peninsula. She herself had been there when she was facing a similar crisis in her vocation and suggested that Shiela fly down there during the Spring break. The winter had been bad that year, and Shiela's parents provided her with the money for the trip during the Spring vacation from school, so that she could consider what she wanted to do with her life.

The woman in charge of the program there in Cozumel spoke to her about discovering the divine within and freeing herself from the entire male establishment. The rest was wonderful. She soaked up the sun, enjoyed the abundant fresh fruits and vegetables, and the charming Mexican music.

Listening to the shaman talk about the Goddess and her power gave her new insights into life and living and enabled her to see herself in a totally different way. In fact, she had never been the same since. When he invited her to receive the initiation and become a priestess of Ix Chel, she responded eagerly. When he told her that he would draw down the moon on her, she could hardly wait for the night when it would actually happen.

Since there were about six women to be initiated at that time and each one was to be initiated separately, she had to wait her turn in great anticipation of the big event. When the night of the full moon finally arrived for her initiation, Ozalie and Lyrica, the women in charge of the retreat house, led her into an inner chamber where there was a pool with a fountain splashing joyously in its center around which floated large water lilies. A white marble statue of Ix Chel stood in the center of the pool and seemed to welcome her into her company. Ozalie gave her an organza robe that was like a blue cloud as it embraced her naked body. Lyrica insisted that when the shaman appeared she was to take off the robe and stand before him totally naked in the waters of the pool.

As she waited there for the shaman to appear, she was utterly exhilarated. The lights were gradually dimmed and then extinguished with only the moonlight shining down upon her, for the glass ceiling had been retracted and there was nothing between her and the moon's rays that gently caressed her body. At exactly the stroke of twelve, thirteen women all completely nude came and cast a circle around her. Ozalie handed her an exquisite athame with a shining silver blade and black ebony handle and Lyrica gave her a wand, also made of silver, and about four feet long. She was to hold the athame skyward in her right hand with the wand in her left.

The thirteen women that encircled her began chanting a litany to the Great Mother Goddess, calling out all her names from Artemis to IX Chel to Peli and so on through the pantheon of ancient Goddesses. They invoked the Goddesses of the air, sky, water, and earth as they splashed merrily in the waters of the pool. As soon as the circle was drawn, the shaman appeared utterly naked. Approaching her and standing right in front of her, he began the ceremony that would dedicate her to Ix Chel and make her a priestess of the Moon Goddess. With a jewel encrusted sword outstretched, he tapped her on each shoulder and held up before her face a large crystal that captured the rays of the moon and focused them into her eyes. Handing her a heavy. gem-encrusted. golden chalice, he urged her to drink deeply of its contents. She took a sip—it was some kind of fruit essence that was sweet and soothing to the palate. Perhaps it contained a psychedelic drug, because she soon began to experience strange sensations. The chanting of the women was hypnotic and at the same time liberating. The shaman whispered that he was getting ready to draw down the Moon Goddess who would possess her body and soul. As he prayed over her, she suddenly felt free of the past, free from all the restraints that the male hierarchy had imposed on her. She was free of guilt and shame and her spirit soared. Most of all she felt empowered by Ix Chel and she knew that she would never be the same again.

As a result of this life changing experience, she returned to the States with new purpose, having come to the decision that she would remain in the Ardorines, but would work for reform and share with others the liberation and power she had found in Ix Chel. Soon she discovered that some of the other Ardorines, also weary of male rule and practices, shared her interest in the Goddess. Before long, there was a coven of thirteen of them at Santiago where they were surreptitiously teaching the children about the Goddess and different manifestations of the Divine Being. She began to read what other women had written of their experiences and learned what it really meant to be a feminist.

Rousing from her reverie, she realized that it was getting late and that she had to be in her office in the school early in the morning. As principal, she had many duties that called for her presence. Although she enjoyed her work, she regretted not being able to teach classes now that she was principal, for she had always enjoyed teaching, especially chemistry and biology.

Putting her meditation aside, she stood up and walked across the stepping stones in the surrounding water to the altar where she blew out the candles that were burning below the icon of Ix Chel. As she made her way to her room, she whispered a good night prayer to Ix Chel and one to Sheela-na-gig with whom she had recently become acquainted. Since the Druidic goddess shared her name, she felt especially drawn to her. After all there was only one Threefold Goddess who manifested herself as maiden, mother, and crone, although she had many names.

3
Father Mel

After a sleepless night, Father Mel rose early and said Mass privately in the rectory chapel, a small room located just off the living room. Before it could be used again, the church would have to be re-consecrated because of the murder. He would have to call the chancery and have them make the arrangements.

When he finished the Mass, Nirvana Kobe, the kindly black housekeeper had a big breakfast of pancakes, ham, a New Orleans style omelet with creole sauce—her specialty—with biscuits and red-eye gravy waiting for him on the buffet in the dining room.

"Morning, Father," Nirvana greeted him with a cheery smile. She always reminded him of Aunt Jemima with her hair tied up in a bright red bandana, just like the smiling woman on the box of pancake mix. From her looks, it was easy to see that she enjoyed pancakes and other fattening foods.

"Morning, Nirvana," he replied as he poured a cup of coffee. Although he was not at all hungry, he nibbled on a biscuit with honey and drank some of the heady brew with chicory that Nirvana had placed in a pot on the buffet. As was her custom, Nirvana went to the front door and retrieved the *Rosanada News* from the porch, where the boy had thrown it. When she opened the paper and glanced at the front page, she let out a holler.

"Mercy, Lord! It says here that someone killed Sister Megan in the sacristy last night?" When she handed him the paper, he laid it down on the table beside him without looking at it. From his place at the head of the dining room table, he could observe Nirvana who had rushed to the kitchen. Quickly she lit a candle and placed it before the statue of Our Lady of Mercy that she kept on a shelf above the kitchen sink. Deeply agitated by the news of the murder, she was wringing her hands and daubing her forehead with a handkerchief that she kept rolled in a ball in her left hand. Crossing herself quickly, she came and stood in the dining room doorway.

"O Father Mel, I just knew that something terrible was going to happen when I had that dream last night about black vultures flying around here. I said to my chaps, 'There is bad news in store for the church. Mighty bad.'"

In all the time she had worked in the rectory, he had never seen Nirvana so distraught before. "Don't worry, Nirvana. They will catch the killer and put him behind bars. God is in control. He will take care of us." Although he was trying to reassure her, his words sounded like tinkling brass.

"I don't like working where there's killing going on. Perhaps I should…"

Not wanting to lose his housekeeper, Father Mel opened his wallet and pulling out a fifty dollar bill, gave it to her saying, "I am giving you a raise, starting right now. Will that help make you feel better?"

"Oh, Lordie, yes, Father Mel. Thank you." With a big smile, Nirvana took the money and put it in her apron pocket and returned to the kitchen, humming to herself.

Just as he was finishing his second cup of black coffee, Monsignor Petit entered the dining room and took his place across the table from him. Father Julian was still in church where he always said the Mass at seven every morning.

"Good morning," Monsignor Petit grumbled as he poured a cup of coffee from the coffee pot on the buffet and put a small portion of the omelet and ham on his plate. In no mood for conversation, Father Mel was glad that Monsignor was not garrulous and was content to eat in silence. Each of them retreated into his own thoughts and Father Mel opened the *Rosanada News* that Nirvana had given him and was confronted by the story of Sister Megan's murder, as Wayne Creasy had pieced it together from the police records.

Nun Murdered in Sacristy
Wayne Creasy

Sister Megan McGrath, teacher at Santiago parochial school was found dead in the sacristy of the church last night about 11:00 p.m. by Rev. Malleus Shamrock, the pastor. She was brutally killed by an unusual pole with a very sharp tip that pieced her heart and by a strange knife that was plunged into her lower abdomen, piercing her uterus. The police are investigating and hope soon to have some insights into this bizarre crime that has the appearance of a cult assassination.

Unable to continue reading, Malleus tossed the newspaper down beside him on the table and started to get up, just when the door bell rang and Nirvana shuffled to answer it. From where he sat in the dining room, Mel could not see who entered the house, but he could hear Nirvana, speaking to the visitor.

"Come on in, I'll call the pastor. Go right on into his office and he will be with you in a minute."

Laying his linen napkin down beside his plate, Father Mel pushed his chair into the table and went into the office that was just was opposite the living room. At once he recognized Cristian Forte's sister who was waiting eagerly to see him.

"Good morning, Mrs. Patinho."

"It's Ms Forte, Father," she said firmly.

"Isn't Roberto Patinho your husband?" He looked at her quizzically and saw that she appeared annoyed with the way he had addressed her.

"Yes," she quickly explained, "he is also my law partner, but I go by my maiden name. Our firm is Forte and Patinho. But I did not come here to talk to you about that." He could perceive that she had a complaint and that was what had brought her to the rectory.

"Please be seated. Well, what did you come to see me about this morning?" Sitting down at his large oak desk, he motioned to the gray leather chair that stood across from his desk.

After putting her trim black leather attaché case beside the chair, she sat down carefully smoothing out her flawless navy blue suit so it would not wrinkle under her. Although she was a beautiful woman, with rich black wavy hair and eyes the color of amber, her approach was strictly business.

"I am here, because I am disturbed about the things my daughter Bella is learning at school from her teacher Sister Diane." Shaking her head sadly, Carla Forte continued: "My daughter tells me that she does not believe in original sin and that the story of Adam and Eve is just a myth invented by men to denigrate women. If fact, she says she does not believe in sin and guilt at all any more."

Mel could see that Ms. Forte was ready to do battle. "Well, I'm glad you came to see me," he said in an attempt to placate her. "I am sure there is some misunderstanding, and I will try to clear it up. Sister Diane is a fine teacher. She got her degree from the state university. She comes to us with the best credentials and recommendations."

Obviously a busy person, Ms Forte was already on her feet and heading for the front door.
"Thank you for your time and help, Father. I knew you would take care of it." With that she left as quickly as she had arrived.

No sooner had Carla Forte left the rectory, when the door bell rang a second time. He could see that it was going to be one of those hectic days that were the rule at Santiago. This time Mel answered the door himself. It was Detective Zadek and a fellow officer.

"Yes, gentlemen, what can I do for you," Mel asked as he let Zadek and the officer who was introduced to him as Detective Rogers into the rectory. He could see from the serious expressions on the detectives' faces that urgent business brought them there.

"Sorry to bother you, Reverend, but I have a warrant to search the premises." He held a paper out for Mel to read. Signaling to his police van that stood in front of the rectory, he motioned for three more men to join him. Like a pack of bloodhounds they descended on the rectory.

"Go right ahead, where do you want to begin your search?" Mel asked knowing full-well that he had no choice in the matter.

"I want to start with the living quarters of your security guard. I believe you told me last night that they are on the third floor? I and my associates here," he indicated the other officers who were standing in a group behind him, "will work as a team. First we will go to Vogel's apartment and then go through the various rooms of the rectory, especially searching your room and those of the other two priests."

"Yes, of course, to reach the living quarters of the security guard we have to take the outside stairway on the back of the rectory to go up there. Come this way." Mel led Detective Zadek and his crew out the front door of the rectory and around the house to the back when they climbed up the wooden stairway that led to the third floor apartment.

When Zadek knocked on Vogel's door and there was no answer, he asked as he peered through the glass pane of the door, "You have the keys, Reverend?"

Mel reached in the pocket of his slacks and pulled out his key ring and opened the door for the police. Since Vogel had moved in about four months before, it was the first time that Mel had been in the small living room, bedroom and a kitchen that comprised the security guard's living quarters. He was totally unprepared for what the officers found in Vogel's living room. On a table in the center of the room, he saw all kinds of knives—a real collection of them. Some had double edged blades like the one that the killer left in Sister Megan, others had single edge blades with strange engravings on their hilts. Mel watched as Officer Rogers dusted them carefully for fingerprints.

Next to the knives, were piles of pornographic photos of women in various stages of undress, engaged in all manner of aberrant sexual behavior with male companions or other women. After riffling through them, Detective Zadek directed his photographer to take pictures of the knives and the pornographic materials. Except for the clutter of knives and pornographic photos, Vogel's living quarters were neat and tidy. His bed was carefully made and there were no dirty dishes in the sink.

As Zadek was going through the contents of Vogel's closet, Mel heard footsteps on the stairs leading up to the apartment. Glancing out the door, he saw Valin Vogel huffing breathlessly up the stairs.

"What is going on here?" Vogel inquired with evident displeasure and annoyance, as he entered the apartment and saw Zadek going systematically though his things. "This is private property," he protested. "What right do you have to be here searching my belongings?"

Pulling the search warrant from the pocket of his coat and showing him his police badge, Zadek said, "This is what gives us the right." Then towering over Vogel who was a short, but slim man, he said: "A woman was murdered on these premises. What can you tell me about that?" Putting his badge and the warrant away, he asked: "Where were you last night between eight and eleven?"

"I was right here," Vogel protested loudly. "I was right here watching TV."

"Do you have anyone who can corroborate your story?" Rogers, a short fat man dressed in a plain brown suit, asked as he advanced toward Vogel who was starting to look nervously around the room to see what the police had found.

Picking up a double edged knife from the table, Zadek demanded: "What do you do with all those knives? This one looks just about like the one we found in the murdered woman."

"It is just a hobby of mine. I collect knives, there is nothing illegal about that," he protested as he began to sweat. His face became flushed, as he waited for Zadek to continue questioning him.

"Where did you get this porn? Are you trafficking in porn" You selling the stuff?" Rogers demanded getting right up in Vogel's face.

"No, I just bought it. I'm an adult. Surely it is not against the law to have a few girlie pictures…" Vogel dropped down on the sofa and propped his elbows on his knees and sunk his head in his hands and remained gazing at the floor.

"Who did you get this stuff from? If you bought it, surely you can tell me who you got it from," Zadek insisted.

"I got if from Yo-Lin Sin. She has a nude bar up the river...*La Estrella de Amor.* I have gone their a few times to take in the show." Defiantly he looked up at Zadek.

"Yeah, we know her and the kind of stuff she sells. You didn't buy any kiddie porn from her did you?" Rogers demanded aggressively.

"No, no, of course not. I am not into that sort of thing," Vogel protested adamantly. Feeling sorry for Vogel who was under attack, Mel walking to the door said to Zadek: "Would you like me to show you the rest of the house now?"

"Yes, Reverend. Lead the way."

Returning to the rectory downstairs, Mel led them into his office where there was nothing but parish records and a few shelves of theology books—mostly his old text books from the Julius III seminary. Quickly they proceeded through the living room and the dining room where there were no personal effects and then on into the kitchen.

When they entered the kitchen, Nirvana greeted them with a frown. "There's nothin' in my kitchen, 'cept food and dishes, and pots and pans. And I keep things neat and in order." She glared at them almost daring them to mess up her kitchen.

"Thank you, Ma'am. You keep a fine kitchen. We won't disturb anything. Just want to take a quick look around."

When they finished looking through the downstairs of the rectory Mel led them up the large central staircase that went from the entrance hall up to a landing that contained a massive stained glass window of the crucifixion and then bent backwards, dividing into two staircases that led to the second floor, one on either side of the central stairs.

As the men systematically searched though the contents of his room, Mel observed them in silence. Since his tastes were simple, he had very little to interest them—a CD player and a few CDs, a few books, a couple of clerical black suits, a few pairs of shoes, some black slacks and clerical shirts, and a drawer full of underwear. Satisfied that Mel's room contained nothing to interest them, Zadek said, "I want to examine the old priest's room myself, Is he here?"

"No, he is over in the parish hall, if you want to talk to him," Mel stated in a matter of fact manner.

"No that won't be necessary. Just want to search his room thoroughly. After all he was in the church about the time of the murder, according to what he told me last night. Which room is his?" Zadek asked as the other members of his crew stood waiting for his directions.

"Right here," said Mel, "opening the door into a large bedroom that was lined with bookshelves on one side.

As Zadek began examining the books, he commented, "All in French or Latin." Then he directed the others to go through the drawers in the dresser and the clothes in the closet thoroughly.

A priest of the old school, who had lived for years in North Africa, he had few possessions, and they were arranged neatly in the drawers and in the closet. A man of simple tastes, he obviously lived an austere life. Mel did not think they would find anything in the monsignor's room to tie him to the murder.

After the police had carefully searched everything in Monsignor Petit's room to their satisfaction, they examined the contents of Father Julian Parnell's room, but finding nothing sinister or suspicious there either, Zadek led his crew down the staircase stopping on the landing to speak to Father Mel as he stood in front of the stained glass window of the crucifixion. Taken by complete surprise as he was waiting to escort the police from the rectory, Father Mel, listened in disbelief as Zadek who towered above him, since he was over six feet tall, looked down at him and with eyes like flint said:

"Malleus Shamrock, I am booking you on murder charges for the murder of Megan McGrath. I will have to take you into the station with us."

Mel could not believe what he was hearing. "I don't understand, Officer." Without further explanation, Zadek Immediately began reading him his rights. "You have the right to remain silent. Anything you say can and will be used against you in a court of law. You have the right to speak to an attorney and to have an attorney present during any questioning. If you cannot afford a lawyer, one will be provided for you at government expense."

Stunned by this turn of events, Mel exclaimed emotionally, "Yes, I will phone him at once. Might I ask why you are charging me with the murder of Sister Megan?" Mel demanded insistently.

"Your fingerprints were on both of the murder weapons. We know they were your prints, because the chancery faxed me your prints and those of the other two priests that live here. As you know they keep all priests' fingerprints on file. I got them the first thing this morning and yours match the prints on the weapons that killed the nun." A look of smug self-satisfaction registered on Zadek's irregular features.

His head spun. He felt dizzy and numb. It was a nightmare and Mel found difficulty in believing that it was actually happening to him.

"Let me call my lawyer." Since Ms. Forte just left it was natural for him to remember that her brother Cristian Forte, the detective that solved the Chancery Murders, was now a criminal attorney. He gave him a call and arranged for him to meet him at police headquarters within the hour.

Upon hearing from Nirvana that officer Zadek had returned to the rectory, Monsignor Petit came into the living room just as the officer was putting the handcuffs on Mel. A well-experienced priest and pastor he sized up the situation and said,

"Don't worry, Father, I'll take care of everything here. I will call the chancery and arrange for the church to be re-consecrated. I will also arrange for your bail and get you back home here as soon as I can." The old priest patted him on the shoulder to reassure him.

Confident that he was dealing with a savage murderer, Zadek directed Mel to put his hands behind his back so he could put handcuffs on him and then snapped shackles on his legs and led him to the patrol van that was parked at the front of the rectory.

"Sorry, Reverend," You'll have to get in the back," he commanded while opening the back door of the van and waiting for Mel to climb him.

When they arrived at the headquarters of the

Rosanada Police Department, Zadek led him, shackled and handcuffed, from the police van into the station. Temporarily, they put him in a cell with three other men who were waiting to be booked. When the other men in the cell saw by his black suit and Roman collar that he was a priest, they began to curse him.

"One of them faggot priests!" sneered the biggest of the three men, a burly man of about forty. Doubling up his fist, he smashed Mel in the face, knocking him to the floor. Instantly the other two men jumped on him and began kicking him. Pain ripped through his chest. He felt like they had broken a rib.

"You're nothing but scum, you dirty priest," one of them yelled, kicking him again, as Mel lay doubled up in pain on the floor of the cell. Fortunately a jailer heard the commotion, came running, and summoned help. Quickly they pulled the attackers off him and took him into a private cell where he waited for a doctor to treat his injuries.

4
Cristian Forte

At the breakfast table finishing his morning coffee, Forte who was reading Wayne Creasy's item in the *Rosanada News* about the brutal murder of Megan McGrath at Santiago Church was not surprised when the phone rang and it was Father Shannon.

"This is Father Mel. I need your help, Cristian." His voice was laden with anxiety.

"I just read about the murder in the *Rosanada News*. What can I do for you?"

"I am being held at the city jail. They beat me up!"

"Who? The police?"

"No, some of the other jail inmates. When they saw my clerical collar they knew I was a priest and they thought I was being arrested as a sex offender—a pedophile. So they beat me up. The police are charging me with murder," Mel explained in a deeply emotional voice.

"I'll be right there, Father. Don't worry. And don't answer any questions until I get there. I will take care of everything."

Quickly Forte punched the number of his office into his cell phone. Jiao, his secretary and paralegal answered on the second ring.

"I'll be a bit late coming into the office this morning. I am meeting with Father Shannon at the city jail where he is being held, charged for murdering the McGrath woman in the sacristy at Santiago. You know how to get in touch with me, if you need me." He could rely on Jiao Chulee Wong. A beautiful woman, she had studied law at New York University and was an excellent bloodhound once she got on the scent of a crime.

"Anita," he called to his wife who was in the back yard of their Cape Cod home supervising the twins Rodrigo and Juanita, named after their grandparents on his side of the family. The four year old twins kept his wife quite busy. Since they were born when Anita was forty and their son Miguel was a Freshman in college at the state university, the twins were really a second family for them.

Sticking her head through the kitchen doorway, Anita, asked: "You called me?" She was holding the twins, one by each hand as they pulled to return to their play.

"Nothing special, Just wanted to say goodbye. I'm leaving now." Throwing her a kiss, he picked up his briefcase and in minutes, was speeding in his Lexus into the city.

When he met with Father Mel, he was not prepared for what he saw. The priest had bandages on his face, one arm in a sling, and was limping. Slowly and obviously in great pain, he hobbled over to one of the straight wooden chairs and took a seat at the plain oak table—the only furniture in the room.

"What have they done to you?" Forte exclaimed putting his arm around Mel's shoulder and embracing him gently.

"They put me in a cell with three other men. When they saw that I was a priest, they attacked me calling me "Faggot priest and Chester. They beat me up. Thank God, nothing is broken."

Father Mel managed a weak smile, despite his pain. "They are accusing me of murdering Megan McGrath. It is incredible."

"As I advised you on the phone, do not answer any questions. I will handle everything. I will get in touch with Monsignor Petit and help him with raising the bail, as soon as you are arraigned. We will have you out of here within the week." Forte could see that Father Mel was discouraged by the news that he would be in jail for perhaps a week. "Now, tell me what you know about the death of Megan McGrath."

Father Mel sighed deeply. "I know absolutely nothing. I was the one who discovered her body. I have no idea who would want to kill her." Deep creases wrinkled the brow of the priest. Forte could see great anguish reflected in his troubled blue eyes.

"Don't worry, Father Mel. I will put Gian Perdini, a private eye that works for me on the case. He is the very best. And don't worry about legal fees. We will work something out."

When he left the jail, Forte went directly to his office on the thirtieth floor of the glass tower overlooking the Rosanada River, determined to get to the bottom of the case. He punched Perdini's number into his cell phone. "Gian, I want you to get all the information you can all personnel at Santiago—background checks, social security numbers, credit records, bank records, and anything else you can come up with."

"Sure, Boss. If there is any funny business going on there, I will do my best to root it out."

"It might not be as easy as you think, Gian." Forte was certain that some intricate evil had invaded the parish. He was even more sure of that when he learned that the autopsy done on Megan McGrath revealed that she was about three months pregnant. The knife that was buried in her womb was obviously targeting the unborn child within her. The strange pole with the red streamers and beads that pierced her heart reminded him of cult slayings he had encountered in his practice of criminal law.

5
Ariel Ezechiel Zadek

His ambition driving him relentlessly to succeed, Ariel Ezekiel Zadek was determined to ferret out Megan McGrath's killer. With a master's degree in Criminology from the University of Rosanada, he was well equipped to do the job. His family—Ashkenazi Jews—had escaped the Nazis when they invaded the Ukraine in 1941 with their Operation Barbarossa. Since they were jewelers they were able to conceal much of their wealth in gems sewn in their clothing, when they paid off the authorities and escaped to relatives in Switzerland, and from there to New York. One of their sons, Zeek's grandfather became a rabbi, having studied at Hebrew Union College. Moving to Rosanada, he ministered to the people at Rosanada Chabad, the local liberal synagogue, After his grandfather died, his grandmother moved in with Zeek's dad, a financial consultant, where she still lives being in advanced age.

With search warrant in hand, Zeek kissed Margie, his live-in girl friend, good bye, thanked her for fixing a nice roast beef dinner, and took the elevator to the basement of the building where his steel gray Toyota was parked. Having no children, they lived in a small apartment in the center of Rosanada in the First National Bank Building, overlooking the Rosanada River. Perhaps, he figured, he would turn up something in the dead girl's room at the convent of Santiago that would lead him to the killer and help bring him to justice.

When he arrived at the convent about eight in the evening, Sister Shiela whom he had previously encountered, opened the door for him. Earlier in the day he had searched the rectory and was returning with Detective Rogers to see what they could uncover now in the convent.

"Good evening, Detective," Sister Shiela said very brusquely. "We are busy now. We don't have time to talk." She started to close the door in his face.

"Wait!" he commanded. "I have a search warrant."

Heaving a deep sigh, Shiela said with annoyance, "Of course, come in, Officers. What do you want to search? Our chapel? Our dining room?" Speaking sharply, she clipped her words sarcastically.

"First of all, I want to look around the entire convent and especially see Sister Megan's room and her personal effects," Zeek insisted holding out the search warrant for her to see.

Amazed at the chapel with the rushing waterfall and icon of Ix Chel and the pool surrounding the altar, Zeek could only stare in silence, while Sister Shiela impatiently waited for him to move on to the other rooms of the convent. As they went from bedroom to bedroom, he observed the sisters at their desks getting their lessons ready for the next school day. When they came to an empty bedroom, Shiela turned on the ceiling light saying, "This is Sister Megan's room."

Very systematically Zeek and Rogers began going through Megan's personal things, unfortunately finding very little that would help further their investigation and convict Shannon. She had the usual things one would expect to find in a young woman's room, but not the kind of things he would expected a nun to have. There were no prayer books or rosaries and from what he had heard they were the stock in trade for nuns. He was surprised by the extent of her wardrobe. Frilly blouses and ruffled skirts hung in the closet. There was a furry white parka and tall leather boots that went up to the knees. In one of the drawers of the white French Provincial dresser, he discovered black lace underwear similar to what she was wearing when she was killed. When he saw lace nightgowns in black, green, red, and white piled high in another drawer, Zeek decided that Megan must have spent all her money at Victoria's Secret. The only thing that spoke of any kind of religious devotion was a small feminine statue that stood on the bedside table. He figured that it was a statue of the Virgin Mary, until he read the words "Ix Chel" on the base and "Hecho en Mexico" on the bottom. The name Ix Chel sounded to him like an Indian name—Mayan or Aztec.

When he spotted a personal computer on Megan's desk beside the large casement window overlooking the street, he hasted to examine it. Looking at the machine carefully without touching it, Zeek asked Sister Shiela who had been following his every movement with gimlet eyes as he searched for evidence:

"What did she use the computer for?"

"Each of us has her own personal computer in her

room for doing school work, of course," Shiela replied annoyed that he was lingering in Megan's room and anxious to terminate his visit so that she could go on about her business.

Returning her penetrating stares, Zeek informed her: "I will have to take this computer hard drive with me." he said as he quickly scribbled something on a pad he was carrying with him, ripped off the top sheet, and handed it to her.

Snatching the paper from him—-it was a receipt for the hard drive—she asked with ice in her voice, "Will that be all, Detective?"

"It is all for now, but I will be back," he replied adamantly with a look of determination in his steel blue eyes. As he lingered in the hallway outside Megan's room, Shiela motioned impatiently for him to leave.

"I'll see you out now," Shiela said firmly as she proceeded down the stairs to the first floor with him at her heels. Opening the front door, she motioned for him to go.

As he drove back to the Rosanada Police Department with Detective Rogers, Zeek decided that there probably would not be anything of value on the computer, but he wanted to check to be sure. Once back at headquarters, he took the machine into the computer department and asked tech support to see what they could find on it. They would let him know when they had the results.

6

Shiela

Completely overcast with dark clouds constantly threatening rain. It was a horrible day for a funeral. Although the entire parish was under a pall, the lay people, especially the women of Santiago, came to celebrate the passing of Sister Megan and give her a good sendoff. All the sisters were terrified as they stared in disbelief at her slender body lying in the convent chapel at the foot of Ix Chel's icon, before being taken to the church where Father Julian preached a lovely homily, saying he was sure that Megan was in heaven among the blessed. There was a large turn out of parishioners, especially the women, who always showed their support for the convent and its nuns. After the final tolling of the bell, Megan's body was hurried away in a sedate black hearse to be shipped to Pennsylvania where the provincial had arranged burial in the cemetery there in the rolling hills of the Allegheny mountains, the American home of the Ardorines. Mother Provincial had assured her that another sister would soon come to Santiago to teach the second grade.

Night had fallen, and Shiela was sitting in the convent chapel before the icon of Ix Chel, meditating on the events of the day. To lift her mood and brighten her spirits, she had taken many floating candles that were made to resemble water lilies and lit them and placed them on the waters of the pool surrounding the altar. The flickering flames soothed her troubled spirit as she cried out in the depths of her heart to the Goddess. Her heart ached for Megan; she was so young to be ripped from this life. Why couldn't have she been more careful? Why did she have to put herself in such a position that her death was the only solution? She wasn't the first nun to get pregnant. She had tried to arrange for her to have an abortion. Abortion would have solved everything. She thought about the brave nuns who had taken out a full page ad once in the New York Times, stating their names, and professing that it is a woman's right to choose and to abort an unwanted embryo. After all it was just a blob of tissue invading a woman's body. Monsignor Petit had seemed shocked when he related the news to her that the autopsy had revealed that Megan was eight or ten weeks pregnant. Of course, he was of the old school.

In the candlelight, the painting of IX Chel seemed to come alive behind the splashing cascades of the waterfall that flowed from around her and bubbled into the waters of the pool. As she continued her thoughts, some of the other sisters came and joined her in the chapel. Shiela watched as one by one they came in, dipped their fingers in the water of the pool and splashed it on their faces while bowing before Ix Chel. Then each of them threw a few grains of incense on the burning embers of the eternal flame under the bronze laver where a fragrant jasmine potpourri, sacred to Ix Chel, bubbled and simmered. When Sister Lotta came to the chapel she sat down at her harp and began to play her heavenly music that always calmed and soothed Shiela when she was distressed.

When her cell phone started vibrating in her slacks pocket, Shiela quickly left the chapel and took the call in the convent living room that had become chilly, because the logs in the fireplace had burned out leaving nothing but a few embers. A wonderful feeling of relief took possession of her as she recognized the familiar voice of Mother Provincial.

"I called to give you my condolences and offer you what comfort I can during this trying time," Mother Brunhilda said softly.

"It is so nice of you to call, Hilda," Shiela replied. "You are always so thoughtful."

"I have a new sister who will fit into your circle very compatibly. Sister Rose is a very willing learner. She is quite young, and this is the first time I have sent her out on a teaching assignment. She is trained in all the basics and is a budding feminist who is eager to learn more about the things that are so important to you and the rest of the sisters at Santiago. You can have the pleasure of training her."

"Thank you, Hilda. We will do our best. You can be sure we will receive her with open arms."

"She is going to arrive tomorrow. Please pick her up at the airport at 3:45 pm. She is coming on Cross Country Air on CCA flight 314."

"Of course, Hilda. I will send one of the sisters with the van to meet her. We will put her in the guest room."

"May the Goddess bless you, Shiela. Good bye."

With Sister Rose joining the coven, they would be able to resume their liturgical practices that always require a full coven of thirteen. Hoping that the arrival of Sister Rose would help to restore the spirits of the sisters in her care, she turned out the lights in the living room and went to her room.

Quickly undressing, she slipped into a pink satin nightie, pulled down the covers on her queen-size bed, and stretched out, hoping to find sleep and restoration for her weary spirit. The past few days had been extremely trying. As she lay their in the darkness, the light outside her window cast strange shadows into her room. She could hear the clock ticking on her desk beside the bed. Sleep eluded her. "Oh, Ix Chel," she prayed, "hear and come to my aid." But Ix Chel was deaf to her prayers. When sleep finally came, disturbing dreams afflicted her.

She dreamed she was in Mexico on the Island of Cozumel. The full moon overhead lit her path as she walked barefoot on the beach with the warm waters of the sea caressing her steps. Suddenly a cloud covered the face of the moon, when a shaman appeared dressed in a goat skin, wearing horns on his head. Taking her by the hand, he led her dancing into the dark waters that lapped upon the shore. As they went farther and farther into the surf, she tried to break lose from his grip, but he held her fast. Higher and higher rose the waters about her, submerging all but her head. Violently, she pulled to free herself from his embrace, as he took her into his arms and held her fast with the ink-like waters now beginning to wash completely over her. Gasping for breath, she cried out, "Ix Chel, save me! I am drowning!"

As she sank into the depths of the sea, she seemed to hear a strange diabolical laugh, and woke with a thud. Death clung to her in the night, but she broke free, turned on the light beside her bed, and snapped on her television, determined not to yield to dreams and fears.

7
Bishop Renato Del'Ano

Renato Del'Ano dressed carefully putting on his best Italian suit, as he got ready to leave Casa St. Popola where he had a large suite on the top floor next to Bishop Bugumil's. The two of them had become good friends, since he moved next door to him after the horrendous murder of Archbishop L'Abbadon and the arrival of Archbishop Fuchs in Rosanada. He looked forward to dinner with the archbishop. Johannes Joachim Fuchs—Hans to his friends—had taken a firm hold on the archdiocese. With his European background he had transformed Rosanada into a place of culture and erudition. A native of Cologne, he attended the University of Bonn where he got a Th.D. in theology and a Ph.D. in Comparative Religion. After completion of his studies at Friedrich Wilhelm's University, he became a professor of the Catholic seminary in Vienna and a protégé of the Cardinal Archbishop of Vienna, Hartmut Niklaus Bauer, who later became head of the Congregation of Bishops in Rome. From Vienna, Fuchs moved to California where he became an American citizen and dean of the theology department at the prestigious Sasaulito University, until he was named Archbishop of Rosanada.

Looking forward to a delightful evening during which he hoped he would further his career, Renato jumped into his silver gray Maserati grand coupé that was parked behind Casa St. Popola and took off. Since his investments had been doing well, he decided to buy the Italian car he had always dreamed of owning, ever since he was a boy in Torricella. He loved the rich leather interior and the electric seat warmers that made it so cozy in winter. Revving up the engine, he sped from the parking lot and headed for 7 Coziness Lane in the Champs de Bauchery section of Rosanada. As he took the river road, the weather was nippy, below freezing, and there was a bit of fog in the air.

As he drove, he reflected that he would have to be careful with his conversation. Hans—the archbishop insisted that he call him Hans—was dominated by liberal ideas that were hard for him to take. A few snow flakes were beginning to fall, when he pulled into the driveway at the mansion and parked his car next to the archbishop's Mercedes.

When he stepped out of the car, he glanced in the direction of the Olympic size swimming pool that lay behind the house. Every time he saw the pool, he remembered the awful experience he had had when he discovered the body of Jan Zagan floating there. Hurrying past the pool, he entered the house through the kitchen door.

Trudi and Fritz, the German couple that lived in the house and took care of housekeeping and the meals were busy working in the kitchen preparing the dinner.

"Good evening, Trudi and Fritz," Renato greeted

them. "Are we having *Sauerbraten* tonight?"

"Jawohl," Herr Bishof," Fritz said as he took Renato's top coat and put it in the closet where guests' things were kept.

"*Und rot Kohl* and green beans with *spätzle*," Trudi added beaming with pleasure.

Although Renato was not fond of German food, patting Trudi's arm as he walked past her, he said, "Well I hope we are going to have some of your apple strudel for dessert."

"*Der Ärzbishof* is waiting for you in the den. Go right ahead in—you know the way."

Renato walked through the dining room and saw that the table was set with exquisite Meissen china and heavy Swedish crystal. The crystal chandelier and matching candleholders— probably brought over from Austria— were magnificent. As he walked around the indoor pool that separated the dining room from the living room, he observed that Hans, a practical man, had turned it into a fish pond. In the center of the pool a fountain splashed merrily in a burst of color, illuminated as it was with cascading miniature laser optic lights. All manner of exotic fish were swimming among the water lilies that bloomed on the surface.

As soon as he entered the living room, Renato's eyes sought out the wall where L'Abbadon's painting used to hang. Now a large painting by Gustav Klimt was there instead. The painting of L'Abbadon was one of the first things that Hans Joachim got rid of when he took possession of the house. They had tried to raffle it off, but unfortunately no one wanted it, and so they moved it up into the attic of the mansion where it probably still remained.

Gone was all the Oriental furniture. Han Fuchs replaced it with elegant European style furniture in muted earth tones that he had bought in Germany and had shipped to Rosanada. Striding quickly across the living room, Renato entered the den.

"*Ach so, Renato, Kommen Sie herein*!" The archbishop shook his hand and motioned for him to be seated. It is good to see you. You are looking well."

"Quite well, Hans."

"Be seated. Here let me pour you a drink." Hans Fuchs picked up a heavy crystal decanter and poured them both a glass of *Aqua Vitae*, a Danish import that he enjoyed.

"I invited you here for dinner so we could have a quiet conversation, get better acquainted, and chat about things that have been happening in the archdiocese."

"What is on your mind, Hans?" Renato sipped the fiery liqueur, toyed with the crystal glass, and sat back in the chair and relaxed. Although Hans had a totally different theological and moral approach to faith, he seemed to like him, probably because he was always docile and submissive to his authority, and for this reason Fuchs had elevated him to the episcopacy shortly after he arrived in Rosanada.

"I was concerned about the murder that took place at Santiago—that nun—what's her name. *Oh, ja*, Sister Megan McGrath. What can you tell me about the pastor there—Father Malleus Shamrock?"

"Well some years back, a certain fifteen year old

named Bob Reilly accused Shamrock of molesting him. The young man went to his pastor Monsignor Santiago Menor at St. Colon's and lodged a complaint against him. Then Reilly actually came to the chancery and talked to Zagan— he was VG at the time—about it. I checked in Zagan's file and there was no report made of the incident and he did not notify the police. We moved Shamrock from St. Colon's to St. Dymphna's in Daftmarsh, where he was parochial vicar."

"St. Dymphna's in Daftmarsh? Isn't that the rundown parish you closed a few years ago? Hans drained the *Acqua Vitae* from his glass and set it on the very modern blonde table that sat beside his Scandinavian chair.

"Yes, but Shamrock had absolutely nothing to do with it. At the time that happened, he was in New Orleans at Saints Bacchus and Sergius Institute where we sent him for psychological evaluation." Renato finished his drink and put his glass beside Hans' on the table. It was painful for him to remember those past events.

"And what was the evaluation that was made of him at Saints Bacchus and Sergius?" the archbishop inquired leaning forward in his chair to catch every word Renato spoke.

"They were rather non-committal. They simply said that the results of their examination did not indicate any significant degree of abnormality whatsoever. Consequently, we assigned him as pastor at Santiago where he has been ever since. And I must say that he has been an excellent pastor."

Fritz who served as butler came and announced dinner was served in the dining room. Trudi had outdone herself with the *sauerbraten*, if you liked *sauerbraten*. Actually, Renato found German cooking rather heavy and would have preferred Italian or French cuisine. However he did enjoy the white asparagus soup.

"You have made arrangements to reconsecrate Santiago Church, *nicht wahr*?"

"Yes, Bishop Bugumil will take care of it."

"The police requested fingerprints for the three priests in residence at Santiago. I understand that Father Shamrock's prints matched those on the weapons that killed the nun. Is that right?" Hans leaned forward in his chair intent on hearing every word that Renato would speak.

"Yes, Monsignor Petit phoned me this afternoon. Shamrock has been arrested and is being held at the city jail. Monsignor Petit is working to arrange bail."

"How much is the bail?"

"Four hundred thousand dollars." Renato winced when he said this.

"Does he have an attorney?"

"I understand that Cristian Forte will represent him."

"A good choice. A damn good choice. I have decided to make his sister Carla Forte Patinho chancellor of the archdiocese. An extremely capable woman and it will help our public image to have her as chancellor. We need to promote women. What do you think about that, Renato?"

"You know I always agree with you, Hans."

Trudi's strudel was the bright point of the dinner. Sipping their after dinner cordial, Cherry Heering, a Danish import that the archbishop savored, Hans began a discussion on theology as they adjourned back to the den. Extending to him a box of panatelas, the archbishop asked him quite directly, "Renato, what do you think of same sex unions?"

Having heard that Hans Fuchs favored same sex unions, Renato knew that he would have to give a guarded response to the question, after declining the cigar.

"I see the need for a pastoral solution that would allow them to continue their lives of faith. However, I do not know what the final answer could be. I would have to give it serious consideration, before I could give a definitive answer to that question." Nervously Renato glanced at the archbishop who seemed to enjoy having put his vicar general on the spot.

What do you think, Hans, about same sex unions?" Renato bounced the ball in the archbishop's court.

"I'm not gay, Renato, but I sympathize with those who are. And it would be better for them to be in a permanent union that was sanctified by the Church than to drift from one partner to another." Fuchs seemed to be enjoying testing his vicar general.

"Well, yes, I do see your point," Renato agreed. "However, such behavior has been condemned by St. Paul in the New Testament and by the tradition of the Church."

The archbishop chuckled and commented: "Sure, and it is also forbidden to swear, loan money at interest, and to have earthly riches while slavery is sanctioned. What we need to do is go to the essentials of the gospel message. Don't you agree?"

Before Renato could answer, Hans rose to his feet and invited: "Come, let's go out in the kitchen and get Fritz to make us some of his Viennese coffee to cheer us and warm us up."

Renato followed him through the living room, while glancing at the wall almost expecting to see L'Abbadon's painting hanging there. Although it was long gone, the memory of it and of the former archbishop still haunted him.

"Fritz and Trudi have been with me ever since I taught at the seminary in Vienna. They have been very loyal."

In the kitchen they found Trudi busy making what she said was *Schwartzwälderkirschtorte* for tomorrow's dinner.

"It's the favorite of His Excellency," Trudi explained as she spread the cherries and the whipped cream on the chocolate cake, while Fritz began brewing a pot of coffee.

"Fritz makes the best Viennese coffee this side of *Wien*," Hans said while beaming his approval at Fritz. "The secret of his recipe is that he uses only fresh *Schlagsahn* … how do you call it? Oh, yes, whipped cream. He never uses the stuff in the cans."

Renato had to admit that Fritz did make good coffee. When he finished drinking it, he said good night, and headed back to Casa St. Popola where he knew John Bugumil would be waiting for him to return. He was eager to share with him the news that the archbishop accepted the idea of same sex unions.

8
Monsignor Petit

"*Mon dieu! Zut alors! C'est impossible*!" He slapped his forehead with his hand in a gesture of futility. What was the Church coming to? Father Shamrock was in jail accused of the murder of that young nun. He could not understand why Archbishop Fuchs—no he would never call him Hans—had brought those liberal nuns into the archdiocese. As soon as they started those outlandish feminine liturgies in the church and had involved the laywomen in them, he knew they were headed for trouble. Our mother who art in heaven! *Tiens! Tiens!* Everyone knows that God is Father. Prayers to Sophia! The very idea of it was appalling. Goddess worship!

He had almost raised enough money to get Father Shamrock out on bail. And it was none too soon. After all he had been in jail almost a week. Quickly he flipped through the cards on the indexing system on the office desk looking for the phone number for Teresa Valdés, the president of the pastoral council. As soon as he found it, he punched it into the office phone and sat back in the big black leather chair that was usually reserved for the pastor.

"Teresa Valdés speaking."

"This is Monsignor Petit, I phoned to see if you had

received any further bail money." He waited expectantly for her response.

"Yes, I deposited an extra hundred and fifty thousand dollars in the parish account yesterday afternoon. The parishioners have been very generous in helping with this. I am sure you will have enough to arrange the bail now."

"Ah *merci! Magnifique!* I will go *immédiatement* and get him and bring him home.

Two hours later Monsignor Petit drove up in front of the rectory in his Renault with Father Mel. No sooner were they in the rectory when the phone rang. Jean Wilson, the principal's secretary in the school, sounded frantic on the phone.

"Please, Monsignor, come over here at once. Two of the Sisters are having a fight in the hall right outside the office and I can't find Sister Shiela."

"I'm on my way." Rushing out the door, he ran to the school located on the other side of the convent and across from the parish hall. As soon as he was in the building, he could hear the argument of the two women who were screaming at each other.

"Sister Shiela said I move into Megan's old room, because it is a lot bigger than mine," Sister Christa insisted very belligerently as she forced her face into Sister Diane's.

"No, that is not right. Your room is plenty big enough, I need that room, because I need space for my easel so I can paint," Sister Diane countered back, not budging an inch as Sister Christa who was a good four inches taller than she loomed over her.

From what he could see, it looked like Sister Christa

and Sister Diane were going to start pulling each others hair at any moment. Rushing to where they were, he pushed his way in between them.

"Quiet, Sisters!" he commanded them. "Is this anyway for the brides of Christ to behave? Such a petty argument."

As he could feel the antipathy of both women turn on him, he saw Sister Shiela at the end of the hall charging towards him.

"This is not the Dark Ages," she snapped as soon as she was about ten feet from him. "Don't call us brides of Christ. We are not a harem! And what's more, I will thank you to stay out of our affairs. I am in charge of the convent, not you. The Sisters are my responsibility and I will take care of this situation myself." Shiela folded her arms one upon the other and held them against her chest, as if armed for battle.

"I certainly hope you do. But there is one thing that is my concern, and this is as good a time as any to get it corrected," he said determined to put the women in their place. "One of you has tampered with the lectionary and used white-out to cover over the printed words and has replaced them with inclusive language."

"So?" Shiela asked coolly with an arched brow and a fiery glint in her green eyes. Ready to rally to Shiela's support, the other two nuns both turned on him, taking a hostile stance.

"It is a violation of canon law," he responded leveling an icy glance on the coordinator.

"Canon law!" Shiela exploded. Canon law is a joke! Roman legalism!" She sneered at him and chortled to herself. "It is people that matter, not laws." Turning her back on him and speaking to the two nuns who were agreeing with her, she said in very authoritarian terms, "I will deal with the two of you tonight in the convent. Go back to your classrooms at once."

Glad to leave the school and the nuns, Pierre Petit returned to the rectory, where he found Father Mel in the office going through the mail that had come during the week he was in jail. As he entered the office and took a seat in the gray leather chair usually reserved for visitors, he sighed deeply and said, "We really need to do something about those nuns. Two of them were having a terrible argument in the hall of the school just outside the principal's office. Shiela showed up and bawled me out for interfering in their affairs. That woman is impossible." Monsignor Petit looked to the pastor for some direction in handling the matter.

"I'll have a talk with Sister Shiela as soon as possible."

Monsignor Petit was not convinced that it would do any good.

"Well, this week when you were away, one of them used white-out on the lectionary and put inclusive language in it, although it is contrary to canon law for which they show absolutely no respect."

"As you know, canon law is simply a convenience that the hierarchy invokes to suit their purposes and protect their interests. They abrogate it, whenever they wish. Since they don't respect it, neither do the nuns. Just try to invoke it to protect your interests, and you will see how quickly they nullify it." Mel tore open another envelope and began reading its contents.

"We really need to do something about them," Monsignor Petit insisted.

Laying aside the correspondence, Mel considered the matter a few moments and said, "Perhaps we can take the matter up with Bishop Del'Ano. I don't think he likes the Ardorines any more than we do and maybe even less. Perhaps he can use his influence with the archbishop to get them out of here. However, Archbishop Fuchs is a good friend of the Ardorines' provincial—that is why they are here in the first place. He brought them here.

9
Shiela

Dressed in blue jeans and a red plaid, flannel shirt, Shiela blew the whistle that she kept on a chair around her neck.

"Come on! Let's go, Sisters," she called in annoyance, because Diane and Christa were still not ready to get in the van. Since it was Saturday and they were free for the day, she was going to drive them this morning up to the state park. It was good to get in touch with nature, especially now that the leaves were crimson and gold. Walking through the forests. In the autumn sunshine always reminded her of being in the great cathedrals with their stained glass windows.

Sister Rose, the new sister that Mother Provincial had sent to replace Megan, was already in the van waiting for them. Although she seemed so young and so very naïve, the second graders really liked her. Always willing to take orders cheerfully, she was pleasant enough and quite agreeable.

When all the nuns except Christa and Diane were in the van, Shiela opened the front door of the convent and shooed the stragglers out.

"I get to sit in the front seat beside Shiela today," Christa called out in an emotionally charged voice.

"No, you sat there last week. It is my turn," exclaimed Diane defiantly.

Annoyed with both of them, Shiela interjected with authority: "Sister Rose will sit in the front. You two will go to the back of the van."

Obediently Sister Rose moved to the front seat and the other nuns made room for Christa and Diane in the rear where the two of them bickered the whole way to the state park.

It was wonderful to get away from Rosanada, Shiela thought to herself. Now if they could just have peace. Obviously, they all needed the peace of the forest where they could renew their spirits and drink in the majesty of Mother Earth— Gaia—who manifests the Divine Being who may appear as maiden, mother, or crone.

Since it was autumn, the forest was not crowded with large crowds of people the way it was in summer. They drove down a lane under the tall pines and hemlocks until they came to a picnic area that fronted the park lake. As they got out of the van, Shiela put her arm around Sister Rose's shoulder in a protective and nurturing gesture, certain that Mother Provincial had sent her a sister who would fill the vacant place in their coven. Although all the Ardorines were not feminists, as they were in the Santiago convent, Mother Provincial favored their coven and sent them only the most promising and responsive sisters. She herself would complete Rose's training and induction into the coven's practices. Now that Rose had joined them, they had their full complement of thirteen and could proceed with their full liturgical worship.

Quickly the sisters found a few logs and some smaller

branches of oak and in a few minutes they had a fire blazing.

"Come, let's cast the circle around the fire," Shiela invited. "It is chilly and the fire will keep us warm." Picking up her athame and stang from the portable altar placed in their midst, and as the sisters joined hands, she walked to the center of the circle and stood before the fire where she began casting the circle.

"I, Shiela, priestess of Ix Chel stand transfixed between the worlds of time and eternity. I bless and consecrate this circle to IX Chel, may she bless us and manifest herself to us here today."

Then with her athame and stang raised high in outstretched arms, she danced around inside the circle of the sisters.

Picking up a handful of earth, she went to the northern most part of the circle and casting the earth on the ground at her feet, prayed fervently to the Goddess: "Ix Chel, bless this Earth to your service."

"Bless it and us," the sisters cried out with one voice.

Then returning to the portable altar, she picked up a thurible, put incense in it, and when the smoke was billowing out, proceeded to the East of the circle, swinging the censor, as she blithely danced clockwise.

"Bless this incense, creature of air, Ix Chel."

"Bless it and bless us," responded the sisters jubilantly.

Quickly returning to the altar, Shiela laid down the thurible and picked up a tall, virginal, green candle and proceeded to light it from the log fire that flamed before her. With the candle held high above her head, she danced around the circle clockwise until she came to the southern most point.

"Bless this fire," she prayed.

"Bless it and us," the nuns responded.

Dancing to the western extreme of the circle, Shiela bent down and picking up a bottle of water she had placed there, splashed a few drops westward and exclaimed:

"Ix Chel, bless this water, a symbol of all that is feminine."

"Bless it and us," the sisters intoned with their chanting becoming hypnotic.

Returning to the altar, Shiela began invoking the elements:

"Air, Fire, Water, Earth watch over this rite and protect our circle." As she swung the stang overhead, the little bells that decorated its red streamers tinkled joyfully in the crisp late autumn air. Surveying all the women sitting in the circle around her, she cried out in a loud voice:

"I proclaim the circle is set." Taking a pinch of salt she threw it over her left shoulder while exclaiming, "By the power of Ix Chel, I bind the powers within this circle to come to our aid."

Dancing around the fire, she called out to the Goddess. "Ix Chel, we worship you present in our circle and in our hearts. In you, we are divine. She began chanting her name over and over again, "Shie la, Shie la, Shie la. You are goddess, Shiela."

Rhythmically clapping their hands, all the other sisters began chanting their own names …Chris ta, Chris ta,

Chris ta. Di ane, Di ane, Di ane. With each one calling out her own name, the chanting grew louder and louder, as they all proclaimed their divinity. As they began to dance around the fire in a frenzy of passion, the chanting intensified.

"Let us be renewed in IX Chel," cried Shiela emotionally. Let us embrace each other in the love of Ix Chel." The sisters began hugging each other and kissing one another. Attracted to Sister Rose, Shiela drew her to her breast and kissed her on the lips, delighted that the little rose responded to her kisses. Soon she would have to visit Rose in the privacy of the guest room back at the convent. Actually she was tired of Diane and Christa who vied for her favors.

After closing the circle, Shiela had the nuns unpack the picnic baskets from the van and place them on the table not far from the fire. They had packed all kinds of good things to eat. There was ham from Parma, Persian melon, artichokes, potato salad, shrimp salad, black olives, and many other things. Someone even packed in a tin of sprats in memory of Megan. How she ever ate those sprats was more than Shiela could comprehend, but Lotta ate the sprats with enthusiasm. To complete the feast were lots of hot dogs to roast on the open fire with beer and wine to wash them down.

The ritual of drawing the circle and the chanting had seemed to pacify Christa and Diane who were now walking arm in arm around the picnic table. They all had all found peace and freedom in nature, but far too soon they would return to Rosanada and their daily conflicts which had included the death of Megan. Fear stalked the convent ever since Megan's death. Shiela knew that fear would return to them all as soon as they returned to Santiago.

10

Shiela

Night had fallen and meditating on the events of the day, Shiela was sitting in the convent chapel before the icon of Ix Chel, To lift her mood and brighten her spirits, she had taken many floating candles that resembled water lilies, blossoms sacred to Ix Chel, lit them, and released them on the luminous waters of the pool surrounding the altar. As she cried out in the depths of her heart to the Goddess, the flickering flames soothed her troubled spirit. Her heart ached for Megan; she was so young to be ripped from this life. Why couldn't she have been more careful? Why did she have to put herself in such a position that it resulted in her death? She wasn't the first nun to get pregnant. She had tried to arrange for her to have an abortion. Abortion would have solved everything. She thought about the brave nuns who once had placed a full-page ad in the *New York Times*, stating their names, and professing that it is a woman's right to choose and to abort an unwanted embryo. After all it was just a blob of tissue invading a woman's body. Monsignor Petit had seemed shocked when he related the news to her that the autopsy had revealed that Megan was eight or ten weeks pregnant. Of course, he was of the old school.

In the candlelight, the painting of IX Chel, behind the splashing cascades of the waterfall that flowed from around her and bubbled into the waters of the pool, seemed to come alive. As she continued her thoughts, the other sisters began coming into the chapel to join her. Shiela watched as one by one they came in, dipped their fingers in the water of the pool, splashing it on their faces while bowing before Ix Chel. Then each of them threw a few grains of incense on the burning embers of the eternal flame under the bronze laver where a fragrant jasmine potpourri, sacred to Ix Chel bubbled and simmered.

Wanting to demonstrate channeling for them and the sisters. she had invited some of the most dedicated laywomen to join them for a special event, Teresa Valdés, president of the pastoral council at Santiago, and her two sisters, Inez and Isobel, were very much interested in the craft and were always eager to come to their meetings. And she was equally glad to have them, because if their feminine energies were going to change the world they could not remain bottled up in the convent coven, but had to find their way into the minds and hearts of laywomen and their children. So that she could personally overseer their participation, she had arranged for Teresa and her sisters to sit on cushions near her.

When all the nuns were assembled and sitting in a circle on the cushions on the floor near the pool surrounding the altar, Shiela, dressed in her most diaphanous gown of rose-colored gossamer silk, danced around inside the circle. Then skipping lightly on the stepping stones in the water, she advanced to the altar and with outstretched arms holding up the stang and athame, she began the prayers.

"I invoke the angels to come and seal our circle," she prayed. Then laying aside the athame and stang, she made a bold sweeping gesture with her arms. "Holy angels, I summon you, come and be with us and seal our circle!" Suddenly as if in response to her cry, thirteen white doves began circling overhead and slowly one by one came to rest floating on the waters of the pool.

Holding a crystal bucket filled with water in one hand and a pure white rose in the other, Shiela began lithely skipping from one of the sisters to the next. As she approached each one, she dipped the rose in the water of the crystal bowl and splashed water gently into her face. "May the power and energy of Ix Chel be with you and in you," she cried. When all had been sprinkled, she put the crystal bucket and the rose on the altar, took a pinch of salt and throwing it over her left shoulder, said in a strong voice, "I proclaim the circle is set. By the power of Ix Chel, I bind the powers within this circle to come to our aid."

With looks of great expectation on their faces, the nuns and the laywomen waited for the ceremony to begin. Shiela was glad to see that young Sister Rose sat in the front row eager to hear every word she spoke.

Glancing around the circle of faces until she saw Lotta Bierman, Shiela told them: "Sister Lotta has volunteered to be the medium for channeling this evening. Come here, Lotta," Shiela invited with arms outstretched to receive her.

At once, Sister Lotta responded by coming quietly to

the center of the circle, taking a seat on one of the cushions right in front of her. Shiela had channeled entities into Lotta many times in the past. Karlotte Biermann—Chuck, to her intimates—was a good friend. It was a real asset to have her as a member of the community. A brilliant woman from the Green Mountains of Vermont where her German parents had settled when they came to the States in 1946 shortly after the War, she was a real asset to the community. Among her many gifts, she could prophesy and was often able to foretell the future with surprising accuracy, and she was an excellent harpist.

"Good evening, Lotta," Shiela whispered to the robust, informally dressed nun in gray slacks and a white shirt, who waited expectantly for Shiela to begin the channeling. "Just relax." Handing her a mind expanding drug and a glass of water, she waited for Lotta to swallow the pill. Knowing that it would take about twenty minutes for the drug take effect so they could begin the channeling, Shiela began addressing the coven.

"Friends, tonight thought I would talk to you about St. Joan of Arc. Were any of you aware that she was one of us?" Seeing that no one put up her hand, Shiela continued. "It is true. She was a member of the Dianic cult. That is why they burned her at the stake. It came out very clearly at her trial that she first heard her voices at the fairy tree. From her testimony, it is evident that she considered herself divine, just as we consider ourselves divine. We know that the divine spark is within us. Because she lived in the time of the burnings, she had to be very careful of what she said. She testified that when she wrote something and did not want it to be believed she signed it with the cross—using the cross as a sign to her followers to disregard what she had written. In case you still have doubts, Gilles de Rais, her chosen military escort, was also a member of the Dianic cult and was burned at the stake for the old religion. And now Joan is the patroness of France and highly honored, not only in France but in the entire world. "For her fidelity to the old religion, she is truly a great inspiration to us all."

Surveying the faces of the sisters and the three laywomen who were avidly listening to her, she addressed them solemnly: "Although we will never be called on to be burned at the stake like Joan, we must be willing to spread the knowledge given to us. In time the organized religions will dissolve just like the Soviet Union did. Our feminine energies will prevail and give birth a new society. Each one of us can become christ or christa. As Carl Jung says we must find the divine spark within ourselves. We must know ourselves. Ignorance of self is the greatest evil. We must fight it with enlightenment. There is no sin; there is only ignorance." She smiled at the women and observed them to see the effect her words were having on them. Satisfied that they were responding well, she continued:

"We look forward to a global government and a global spirituality. Ecology of Mother Earth, Gaia, is extremely important. Every plant, every animal has as much right to exist as people do. All life is filled with the divine energy. If we don't mend our ways now, we will be faced with a severe ecological crisis. The hole in the ozone at the South Pole keeps getting larger and larger.

The seas are dying,

"Now I will give each one of you secretly the mantra for our centering prayer. The Divine Mother will hear us and help us heal our ailing world." This said, Shiela walked around the circle whispering the mantra into the ear of each woman.

"Let us repeat the mantra over and over again until Ix Chel hears and comes to us," she encouraged them. Dropping to her knees on a cushion and staring intently at the icon of Ix Chel, she said: "Let us make our minds blank and center them on Ix Chel."

Entering deeply into her spirit to get in touch with the Goddess, she took a large crystal that was suspended on a silver chain around her neck and removing it, held it in her hand before Lotta's face, asking Ix Chel to purify Lotta's mind so she could receive the visit of her spirit guide. Instantly Lotta, who was reclining in front of her, focused her amber eyes on the crystal. After a few moments while the sisters were chanting their mantras, she said to Lotta who was responding beautifully to her commands.

"Speak freely to your guide now."

Because she had channeled with Lotta many times, it was easy to establish contact with the supernatural through her.

"Surrender, surrender to the holy presence of your guide," she intoned softly. You are wide awake to the spirit of light that follows you wherever you go," Shiela uttered in a monotone.

Lotta relaxed with eyes closed and her breathing deep and regular. Utter silence fell over the entire group as they expectantly waited, wondering what would happen next.

"Welcome, Ix Chel," Shiela said with the firm conviction that not only the spirit guide would speak, but the Goddess herself would visit them.

In a strange and unknown musical voice, not at all like Lotta's, came the reply. "I am the mother of all that is."

"Welcome, Ix Chel," Shiela repeated and then turning to the various members of the coven and addressing them, she said: "Welcome Ix Chel, all of you. She is here."

A murmur of voices rang out chanting "Ix Chel, Ix Chel, welcome, welcome. Empower us," they begged.

Following a pattern they had established in the past months, everything was going just as she had expected it would.

"Yes," Shiela invited, "Tell us, Ix Chel, about how we can heal and restore our world."

"I am in each of you, speaking to your hearts. I am the one who holds your destiny. Some call me Sophia, others Peli, still others Athena. I am she who is."

Shiela waited, expecting Ix Chel to give them a message as she had done so many times previously, and to heal and help them to rise above the death of Megan.

"Megan," she asked, "is Megan ascending, Ix Chel?"

Suddenly loud vulgar masculine laughter burst from Lotta's throat.

"Stupid woman," the voice yelled. "What do you want?"

A bit frightened by this unexpected turn of events and realizing that an unknown entity had taken over Lotta's body and was speaking to them through her, Shiela was confused and did not know what to do, for such a thing had never happened before. Greatly frightened, she asked the unknown entity cautiously, "Who are you? What do you want?"

"I want to be in you, with you, in your midst. I will teach you the secrets of the universe. I will give you knowledge—great knowledge. You are goddesses and I will teach you to know good and evil," the voice said in honeyed tones. When she observed that Lotta was beginning to thrash about restlessly, Shiela became even more frightened.

"You have nothing to offer to us," Shiela said stamping her foot imperiously. Get out of here, Intruder! Go, at once!" Then in her most cajoling tones, she pleaded, "Ix Chel, please speak to us again!," She could see that the sisters and the laywomen were struck with terror.

"Not that easy, Shiela." When she heard the entity address her by name, icy chills ran up and down her spine.

"Who are you?"

"I am the light bearer. You want light don't you?" the entity asked with a burst of laughter that mocked her.

"What is your name?" Shiela demanded. She did not want to talk to someone she did not know.

"Same old questions, huh?"

"Tell me your name," she demanded.

"I am the Voice of the Night," the entity proclaimed with a loud chortle, seeming to be enjoying himself immensely at her expense.

Suddenly Shiela noticed a strange phenomenon was taking place. A peculiar odor was filling the coven chapel with the smell of rotting flesh. Then a sudden burst of wind extinguished the candles that were burning on the altar before the icon of Ix Chel. A blast of bone chilling cold air encompassed Shiela. It was terrifying.

When Lotta began striking out at her and hitting her in the face with her open palm, Shiela knew she had to do something.

"Take that, Bitch!" the entity cried as Lotta struck her with a doubled up fist. Then a paroxysm of laughter began shaking Lotta violently with her body jerking from head to toe.

"Come back to your senses, Lotta," Shiela commanded, snapping her fingers before her face. She had lost control and the unknown entity had gained total possession of her.

"Do something," Christa screamed.

Help us, Ix Chel," Diane prayed.

Terrified, Shiela watched as Lotta begin writhing on the floor like a snake. A vile stream of curses burst forth from Lotta's lips.

"She is possessed," cried Teresa Valdés. "The devil has possessed her."

Diane and Christa who were seated near her jumped to their feet.

"Do something, Shiela, before someone gets hurt," pleaded Christa with her face twisted in terror.

"Yes, "Diane urged "Let's get help. The devil is loose in this place."

Always in command of any situation, Teresa Valdés,

jumping to her feet, pulled her cell phone from her slacks pocket. "I am phoning Marco Lamadrid. He continues to be a great friend of mine and he is an expert on how to do exorcisms. Her fingers flew over the face of the cell phone as she put in the numbers.

"Reverend Marco, this is Teresa Valdés. We need your help. I am in the convent at Santiago and one of the nuns is possessed, and we are afraid she will hurt herself. Will you come and help us?" Shiela could see the horrible anxiety written on the faces of Teresa, her sisters, and those of all the nuns.

Flipping her cell phone shut, Teresa stuck it in her pocket. "He will be here in thirty minutes," she said confidently. "The interstate highway runs almost directly from Grace Pentecostal Chapel to the Gas'du Hills."

"You are getting a Pentecostal preacher to come here?" Shiela asked in astonishment, as she studied the face of Teresa Valdés that was set with resolute determination.

"He is the one who built Santiago and was pastor here until Archbishop L'Abbadon drove him out of the priesthood. He is the holiest priest I have ever seen," Teresa told them as she began to become calmer knowing that Marco was on the way.

Within thirty minutes, Pastor Marco was ringing the chimes at the convent. By then all the sisters had been dismissed from the chapel, and she and Teresa Valdés were with Lotta in her room. Sister Diane answered the door and ushered Marco quickly to Lotta's bedside.

"Get him out of here," screamed the entity. "You are going to die, Priest."

At once Marco pulled a bottle of Holy Water from the breast pocket of his jacket and began splashing it on Lotta. When it touched her skin, she shrieked with the deep masculine voice that Shiela recognized as the one that had been yelling at them in the chapel:

"I am not afraid of your water and your mumbo jumbo. It will take more than that to silence me."

"Tell me your name. I command you in the name of Jesus Christ of Nazareth." Fearlessly Marco confronted the evil entity that was causing Lotta to thrash wildly around on her bed.

"Abraxas!"

"I don't believe you. You lie. You are not Abraxas. You are not the ancient demon with the head of a king and snakes for feet! I know Abraxas and have fought him, and you are not he. Now leave this woman at once," Marco spoke with authority as he advanced closer to Lotta's bedside and leaned over her.

"I will not go! She is mine," the entity said emphatically as a foul stench of something rotten and putrid began to permeate the room. The odor was so overpowering that Shiela was fighting waves of nausea.

As Shiela watched the girl struggling with the demon, very strangely it seemed as if the features of her face took on a weird altered appearance. Frantically, Lotta was pulling her hair. Her eyes were glazed with a wild look in them, such as Shiela had never seen before in any human being. Rather they were like those of a wild animal—like the eyes, perhaps, of lion or a tiger engaged in a life and death struggle.

Marco held a crucifix up before Lotta's face, and

when she saw it, she let out a piercing wail that was more animal than human. Madly she lashed out at the crucifix, trying to knock it from the hands of the priest.

"*Falso sacerdote, a mí no me gustan tus mentiras! Esta mujer me pertenece*," the entity growled through Lotta in a very menacing tone.

"Does the woman speak Spanish?" inquired Marco, peering intently at Shiela.

"No, she speaks German, but not Spanish." How bizarre it was for Shiela to hear Lotta speaking Spanish. She recognized the language at once because of all the time she had spent in Mexico in previous years.

"More of the tricks of the demon," said Marco bending over Lotta and laying his hand on her forehead. Holding the crucifix in his other hand, Marco spoke firmly and with determination, "I plead the blood of Jesus over this woman. I command you to leave her and this house at once, in the name of the Father and of the Son and of the Holy Spirit. Be gone!"

Shiela was amazed to see Lotta become calm and return to herself She began smoothing out her disheveled hair, and smiling weakly at Pastor Marco, said: "Thank you, I am at peace now."

Shiela escorted Marco to the door. Before he left he studied her face seriously and asked, "Would you mind telling me what you were doing when this entity took possession of the woman?"

"No, not at all. We are into New Age religion and we were just channeling as we have done many times." Shiela replied trying to sound self-assured. "Something went wrong. I don't understand it. Probably some psychological aberration. Nothing serious, I'm sure. She would have come out of it on her own. Sorry to have troubled you and brought you out tonight."

Annoyed that Marco had been able to bring the girl out the trance when she could not, Shiela was anxious for him to leave.

Marco eyed her intently and with his dark brown eyes boring into hers, he exclaimed, "You have not seen the last of that demon. It is not that easy to get rid of them once you have summoned them. Keep a close watch over her. Once he has entered her, he will not leave her until all of you renounce these strange practices. He will not surrender what he considers to be his own without a great fight. Be very careful. She is in great danger. You all are. You will not have peace in this house until you abandon your pagan practices. It is idolatry."

"But always before Ix Chel came to us and taught us beautiful things about life and love," Shiela protested. "Ix Chel is the Moon Goddess of life and love, not fear and death."

"Ix Chel is the same one that calls himself Abraxas. You are playing with fire, Sister, and *will* get burned." Having said this, Marco opened the convent door and stepped out into the night.

Returning to Lotta's bedside, Shiela saw that the nun was peacefully sleeping. Silently she beckoned for Teresa Valdés to turn out the light and leave room. Escorting her to the door, she said to her, "I really wish you hadn't brought him here. It was really unnecessary. I had everything under control. Lotta was just psychologically upset. Probably nothing. If I had felt the need for one of *them* I would have called Father Julian. He understands about us and is sympathetic to our needs."

11

Lotta

She woke with a start. A sudden noise disturbed her sleep. Sitting up in bed, she glanced at the clock on the bedside table. It was midnight— just on the stroke of twelve. Reaching over, she picked up the statue of Ix Chel that stood beside the clock and pressed the figurine tightly to her breast. Just holding it in her hands brought her peace. So that they would all have their very own Moon Goddess, Sister Shiela had given each of the sisters at Santiago a statue of her made of pure white bisque painted with pastel shades that she had gotten in Mexico. "Ix Chel, Ix Chel," she prayed caressing the figurine of the Goddess close to her heart, hoping that the she would speak to her, bringing her the comfort that she so needed.

She could remember nothing of what had happened in the chapel that evening when Sister Shiela had invited Ix Chel to speak through her. When she awoke from the trance, she found herself in her own bed. A strange noise kept intermittently disturbing her. Glancing around the room, she saw nothing out of the ordinary, except that it seemed darker than usual in the corner by the closet. A whirring and a clicking noise that seemed to be coming from the darkness riveted her attention on the dark corner. Then, it was as if, in the darkness, a cloud formed into a churning vortex. She watched as if hypnotized when the cloud took form and began to spin. Out of the spinning vortex, a voice was calling her name, "Lotta, Lotta."

Despite the strangeness of the situation—it was really uncanny—she was not afraid. It was as if she were mesmerized and drawn to the cloud. Then, in the midst of the cloud, a face began to form. Although it was hideous and grotesque, she was attracted to it. "Lotta, Lotta," the voice called insistently.

Slipping out of bed and putting on her slippers, she began walking toward the swirling cloud of darkness. "Come, Lotta," the voice invited. "I am Abraxas. Come to me. You are mine."

Completely spellbound, she walked into the darkness of the spinning vortex. The cloud began to enfold her, drawing her deeper and deeper into its darkness. She found it hard to breathe. She gasped for breath. Just before losing consciousness and falling to the floor, she screamed at the top of her lungs, "Shiela! Shiela."

Her scream seemed to dissipate the cloud that was choking her. Almost instantly Shiela was at her bedside.

"What is wrong?" Shiela asked, helping her to her feet and back into her bed.

"Perhaps it was a dream. I don't know," explained Lotta, placing the statue of Ix Chel back on the bedside table. "I guess it must have been a dream. I saw a face in a black spinning vortex and heard a voice that said he was Abraxas. I don't know any Abraxas. He called me and I could not help myself, I felt drawn to him like a magnet, and then I couldn't breathe, and I screamed," Lotta explained. She had grown calmer now that Shiela had turned on the lights and everything in the room looked normal again.

"Thanks Shiela, I will be all right now," Lotta said. "You can go back to bed. I am fine. Good night."

After Sister Shiela left her room, Lotta was wide awake. Perhaps Father Julian would know how to help with this. He had majored in psychology and sociology at Catholic University and would probably be able to offer some explanation. Digging through the drawer in the bedside table, she found her cell phone and put Julian's number into it. She knew he never went to bed before one in the morning.

"Father Julian." He answered on the first ring.

"Julian, I had the most awful experience. I need someone to talk to.

"What is the problem, Lotta?" They always called each other by first names. That was the trendy thing to do with contemporary priests and nuns.

"It must have been a dream. But I *thought* I was awake." Rubbing her eyes, she glanced in the corner where she thought she had seen the swirling cloud with the hideous face.

"Well, tell me about it," he urged gently.

"I saw this dark cloud with a grotesque face in it and a voice called to me to come and said his name was Abraxas. I got up out of bed and walked into the cloud, and I thought I was going to suffocate. When I screamed, the cloud and the voice both instantly vanished."

"You were probably walking in your sleep."

"The face looked demonic. Wasn't Abraxas the name of an ancient Egyptian demon?" she asked fearfully.

"There are no such things as demons, Lotta. You probably were just sleepwalking. People do that when under great stress. Just take it easy. You were probably upset over Megan's death. Such a tragedy!" His voice was comforting.

"Perhaps you are right," she conceded. "But it was terrifying."

"It you don't feel a hundred per cent better in the morning, come to see me, and we will talk this thing out. I will be at Catholic Charities until four in the afternoon. Then I will be back at Santiago. When you look at this situation in the bright daylight, it will seem different. Good night. May God bless … no," he corrected himself, "may the Goddess bless you."

Finally about two in the morning, Lotta fell asleep again. This time, she dreamed she was running through a dense, dark forest with a huge beast chasing her. It looked like a black panther, but then it changed shape and metamorphosed into a tremendous screeching bird that had the same face that she had seen in the cloud vortex. In the dream, she was repeatedly murmuring the name "Abraxas, Abraxas." The screeching bird changed shape and assumed the figure of a king with a heavy crown on his head, but instead of feet and legs, there were writhing snakes. He drew near to her and clasping her with both hands drew her to himself and kissed her on the mouth. "You belong to me, Lotta. You are mine forever." She melted in his embrace, no longer desiring to flee.

When morning came and she went to her class, she had forgotten the terrors of the night. Julian was right. In the bright morning sun, everything looked different.

12

Father Julian

Preparing to leave Catholic Charities for the day, Father Julian Parnell tidied up his desk, always taking pride that he cleared his desk each day before going home. Never procrastinating, he liked to deal with things immediately, as they came up. Checking to see that all the drawers of his desk were locked, and turning out the overhead light, he closed the office door and headed for the parking lot. His red convertible Monte Carlo was easy to find in the lot. Quickly he jumped in the car, turned on the seat warmers, and headed up the river road in the direction of the Gas'du Hills.

Apparently Lotta had worked out her problem herself, as he figured she would, because she had not phoned him to make an appointment to see him that afternoon. When he arrived back at Santiago, Valin Vogel was busy raking the leaves in front of the rectory.

"Afternoon, Father." Vogel called out to him as he walked from his car to the front porch of the rectory.

"How ya doing, Valin?" he called back.

"I keep busy. Always plenty for me to do taking care of this place, what with the rectory, the convent, the church, the school, and the grounds!" Vogel exclaimed trying to call attention to his importance and his skills at maintenance.

"You do a good job, Valin, keeping the place safe as you patrol the grounds night and day. Not much goes on around here that you don't know about, is there?"

"Nope, I make it my business to keep up with everything, Father."

Once inside the rectory, he decided to have dinner with Father Mel and Monsignor Petit. Although he despised their pious conversation, he did enjoy Nirvana's New Orleans' jambalaya and other Creole recipes. Besides, this evening he needed to remind Father Mel to order some of the special sacramental wine that he always used. He preferred the dark wine to the light that the other priests liked. After dinner, he quickly excused himself and drove to his parents home located on the River Road, actually not far from Santiago.

His parents, Hazel and George, had gone to the desert South West for the fall and winter months, turning their home over to him to use as he wished, knowing that it was better to have the place occupied, rather than vacant. Although he lived officially at Santiago, he spent much of his time in the family home, but he did not keep the staff of servants that his parents usually had when they were in residence.

Pulling into the driveway of their French Provincial home, he noticed that the porch light had burned out, now that it was getting dark early. Well he would fix that.

The main thing he hated about the fall and winter was that he could no longer play golf. Although he was aware that some golfing enthusiasts played in the snow with black balls, he preferred instead to go to his tennis club where he could play indoor tennis year around. He loved sports. He especially looked forward to the snow so he could go skiing up at Jack Rabbit Mountain north of Rosanada.

He loved the family house. Until he went away to Catholic University and Julius III Seminary, it had always been his home. At the university he had immersed himself in psychology, spending hours in the library reading the works of Carl Jung, one of his favorite psychologists. Social work was his second interest in college and that is why he now worked five days a week at Catholic Charities.

For the most part, he found his studies at Julius III seminary tedious and boring, with the exception of Teilhard de Chardin and liberation theology. He admired the priests who went to Latin America and worked with the poor. Marxism had a lot to offer when you came right down to it. Just look at the Castro regime, for example. Castro had worked miracles in Cuba—education and health care were free services for everybody and there were no beggars and no unemployment.

When he entered the house, he hung his coat in the closet, walked into the living room, glancing at the painting of the Matterhorn that hung over the fireplace. Quickly he laid a fire with a couple of oak logs, some small kindling wood, and yesterday's newspaper. Within minutes the blaze caught and radiated its light and warmth into the room. After mixing a pitcher of stingers, he put it and two glasses on the cocktail table in front of the massive overstuffed sofa. Dropping down in the big gold lounge chair before the fire, he reminisced about the events of the day just past. Then he pursued the evening paper and noted that the police were still clueless in finding the one who killed Megan. He also read that the archdiocese was closing two more parishes. All the news was dismal. He read that a certain Father Hobson was being tried for the crime of sexually abusing a ten year old, after first drugging him with a sleeping potion.

Kicking off his shoes and propping up his feet, he was just about to drift off to sleep, when the door chimes roused him. Glancing at his watch and noting that it was exactly eight p.m., he smiled and made his way to the door.

Throwing open the door, he said "Come on in, You are right on time, Shiela." Putting his arms around her tenderly, he embraced her warmly, kissing her passionately on the lips. Out of the corner of his eye, he saw a taxi drive off.

"Good evening," she said. "I brought a few things with me. She handed him her overnight case, which he took in one hand and the pitcher of stingers in the other, and started heading with them up the stairs with Shiela trailing behind him.

When they reached his bedroom he put the overnight case on the luggage rack that was reserved for that purpose. Pouring her a drink and one for himself from the pitcher, he said invitingly: "Here have a drink. I mixed your favorite—a stinger."

She took the drink and sipped it, obviously enjoying it very much.

"Good to see you, Shiela. Let's see what you brought with you."

She smiled at him and waited for him to examine the contents of the bag.

Releasing the clips that held the bag shut, he threw open the lid and began looking through its contents.

"Well, it looks like you are planning to spend the night. You brought your green silk slippers and a beautiful green lace nightie. You always know just what I like." He grinned at her boyishly. Shiela always knew how to do things right. He never had to worry about her getting pregnant. She had an IUD in place.

"How is my Sun God, tonight?" she asked as she began to undress him between sips of the stinger.

"I have been anxiously waiting for my Moon Goddess to arrive. Now that you are here, it seems we will have a perfect evening," he said as he began unbuttoning her blouse.

"I can stay until midnight. Then I have to call a cab and get back to the convent. Four hours should be long enough for whatever you have planned for the evening." She winked at him and grinned back.

"Well, in that case. Let's not waste any time," he said pushing her gently onto his bed.

13
Mel

His ribs still ached from the blows the men at the jail had given him, when they beat him up thinking he was a pedophile. Monsignor Petit had taken care of everything very well during his absence. Because of Megan's murder in the sacristy, the church had been re-consecrated. Coming to his support with the money to get him out of jail on bail, the parishioners at Santiago had been wonderful. Teresa Valdés, a very capable woman, had been especially helpful in raising money. Even Father Julian had been able to get some time off from Catholic Charities to be more available in the parish. He wasn't very good at ministering to the spiritual needs of the people, but psychological counseling was his forte, even if he was filled with liberal ideas. He also helped with paying the bills—always a time consuming job. Although the Mass attendance was a little bit off, outside of that everything seemed fine, with life returning to normal at Santiago, but the police still had no other suspect in the case and the judge had warned him not to leave town.

He was just finishing one of Nirvana's hearty breakfasts, when the office phone rang. Taking his coffee with him, he went to answer it.

"Father Shannon here."

"Good morning, Father," a friendly voice sounded in his ear. "This is Marco Lamadrid."

"Oh, good morning Marco, nice to hear from you. What's on your mind?" Why was the former pastor of Santiago calling? He knew that Marco had been forced out of the priesthood by false accusations made against him. He was familiar with false accusations; he also had been falsely accused, but the accuser had dropped his allegations and after a stay at Saints Bachus and Sergius Institute in New Orleans, he had been reinstated, promoted, and made pastor of Santiago—one of the largest and most active churches in the archdiocese.

"I have a concern and I can't put it out of my mind, so I thought I would give you a call," Marco explained. The other night—I guess it was about three or four days ago, Teresa Valdés phoned me and asked me to come out there. She said that one of the sisters in the convent was possessed. So I rushed out there immediately and did a deliverance of the woman."

"Yes, I know. Do you she really believe that she was possessed?" Father Mel asked with much perplexity.

"Seemed to be the real thing."

"Do you know what caused it?"

"They were channeling. They were trying to get in contact with some Mexican moon goddess—Ix Chel. Very dangerous business. Things got out of control. The medium—a sister Lotta—got rather violent. I thought you should know about it, since it happened at Santiago and you are the pastor."

"Thanks for calling me. Is the woman all right now?"

Mel questioned the wisdom of Archbishop Fuchs in bringing the Ardorines to Santiago. He found their strange liturgies and feminist practices really out of line.

"Well, I was worried, because the entity that was speaking through her left too easily. I am afraid he is still in her and might become even more uncontrollable than he was the other night. I just wanted to warn you so that you could be prepared. If you need me, just give me a call and I will come and help you with it. I have had a good deal of experience with such manifestations."

"Thank you for your call. I appreciate your offer to help. If anything goes wrong, I'll be in touch. Give me you cell phone number, please."

Quickly Mel jotted down Marco's phone number and then dialed the number of the principal's office at the school and hearing the voice of Jean Wilson the principal's secretary on the other end, he said:

"I want to talk to Sister Shiela NOW," he said emphatically.

"Sister is busy right now," the secretary replied putting him off.

"I said NOW."

"Yes, Father."

Almost immediately the nun was on the phone.

"This is Sister Shiela and I *am* busy."

"I want you to be in my office in the rectory in five minutes. Five minutes," he said with authority and hung up without another word.

When the door bell rang, four and a half minutes later, Mel answered the door himself.

"Come in, Shiela," he said walking toward the rectory

office with her following him. Once inside the office, he closed the door behind them and pointing to the gray leather chair opposite his desk, he took his place behind the desk.

"Now I want the details of what happened when you phoned Marco Lamadrid and brought him here the other night." While waiting for her answer, he studied her face that was etched with worry lines, observing that her hennaed hair was a bit disheveled. Chagrined that he had summoned her, her green eyes were defiant as they returned his penetrating stares.

"I did not phone Marco Lamadrid," she said icily. "I don't know him, and I would never have called him for any reason. Teresa Valdés called him." She twisted the ballpoint pen she was holding in her hands, and then stuck it in the pants pocket of her man tailored blue suit.

"And what necessitated her calling him?" he asked already knowing the answer to his question, but wanting to hear it from her.

"Sister Lotta was upset. Just a psychological upset. I didn't think we needed any help. If I had wanted some help, I would have phoned Father Julian. He is excellent at psychology and things of that nature." She twisted rather nervously in the chair as she gave her explanation.

Although she was usually self-possessed and ready to take on any man who tried to cross her or thwart her plans, Mel could see that Shiela was really uncomfortable with the discussion. He pressed his advantage.

"Marco Lamadrid just got off the phone, before I called you. He told me that you were channeling." He put his elbows on the desk and leaned over towards her and looked at here fixedly.

"There is nothing wrong with channeling," she protested now on the defensive. Her green eyes narrowed to slits.

"Ix Chel, the Mexican moon goddess?"

"She is just like one of the saints," she exclaimed boldly. What is the difference between honoring Ix Chel or St. Teresa or any of the other women saints? She guides us and directs us in the paths of wisdom and enlightenment."

"I will not have any channeling at Santiago as long as I am pastor here," Mel proclaimed with all the authority he could muster.

"You have no right to interfere in the affairs of the convent. We can pray to whomever we wish," her voice was rising and so was her temper.

Mel could see that the nun's face was flushed with anger. "I intend to discuss this matter with the vicar general. A nun possessed by demons is a very serious thing. We will see what the VG has to say about it." He knew that Bishop Del'Ano was very reactionary and favored returning to the days of Pius XII. Perhaps he might be instrumental in getting the Ardorines out of the parish.

She was tall—perhaps five feet seven, but he towered over her. Looking down into her face that was twisted with uncontrollable emotion, he said with finality, "That's all. You may go now."

Grimacing, she headed for the door, "You have not heard the last of this," she called out over her shoulder. I will certainly tell Mother Provincial about this intrusion into the affairs of the Ardorines." Slamming the rectory door, she left cursing under her breath.

Perhaps, he reasoned, Monsignor Petit or Father Julian might have some ideas about how to deal with the Ardorines. As soon as they had taken their places in the dining room for one of Nirvana's Creole suppers, he was anxious to broach the subject with them over dinner. No one could fry catfish and hush puppies the way she did. Even Monsignor Petit, who did not enjoy Louisiana cooking very much, was enthusiastic about her catfish and hot sauce. Always very supportive of what Mel was trying to accomplish in the parish, Monsignor Petit was a welcome addition to the staff at Santiago, for Mel could rely on him since his opinions were sound and reliable and his judgment rock solid.

"The nuns have been channeling and have run into some problems recently," Mel said in a rather non-committal tone, as a way of starting the conversation.

"What happened?" Monsignor Petit asked, taking a sip of the California Sauterne.

"Yes, tell us about it," Julian prompted, as he served himself a serving of collard greens.

"From what I heard, they were trying to channel down a Mexican moon goddess—one of those feminist things—and instead they got a masculine entity that frightened them out of their wits," Mel explained.

Teresa Valdés called Marco Lamadrid to help them. Apparently he brought the nun out of her trance and banished the evil spirit."

"Oh, come on, surely you don't believe in demon possession," Julian remarked as he set down his knife and fork and looked at Father Mel attentively as he waited for a response.

"I am just telling you what Marco Lamadrid told me on the phone awhile ago. He was concerned that the entity would return," Mel explained.

"Channeling is harmless," Julian insisted. "Carl Jung, the great Swiss psychologist engaged in much channeling," Julian said as he took a second piece of catfish from the platter and helped himself to a serving of yams. "The New Age is deeply into channeling. It is a widely accepted practice."

"Yes, I have read about Carl Jung. He had many troubling experiences with poltergeists— pranksters that played tricks on him, like pulling the covers off his bed at night," Monsignor Petit said as he looked askance at Julian.

"The main thing is that the woman, Sister Lotta, responded abnormally and all the women who witnessed the event were frightened," Mel stated flatly. "I plan to discuss it with Bishop Del'Ano. I know he does not approve of New Age practices. I wish the archbishop had never brought those nuns here." Mel laid his napkin down on the table and waited for Nirvana to clear the dishes and bring in fresh baked pecan pie.

"Oh, I think the Ardorines are great," Julian exclaimed. "I like their feminine liturgies and their ideas about the femininity of God. I think they are doing a great work teaching the school children these New Age practices. Hopefully this generation of children will grow up without a Catholic guilt complex." He smoothed his curly blonde hair back from his face, and with a twinkle in his blue eyes, remarked," Sister Shiela is a very talented and capable woman. I would trust her any day."

Unconvinced Mel looked at Monsignor Petit and remarked, "The nuns are skating on very dangerous ice."

14

Zeek

When he arrived at police headquarters there was a memo from the computer tech men waiting for him, telling him to stop by their office that they had some important information for him. Immediately he dropped everything and raced to get the results.

"I think we found what you were looking for, Zeek," the tech, a computer nerd with thick lenses, told him. "Here sit down at this computer and I will show you. I have also made a print out of all we found, and I will give it to you."

As the tech flicked on the power switch and the monitor, Zeek sat down at the machine and waited as the Windows program loaded. Then the tech proceeded to show him the documents that Megan had stored in Microsoft Word. There were lesson plans for her classes, her grades for all her pupils in all subjects, and a tedious document about some Ix Chel down in Mexico.

"Not much of interest I am afraid," Zeek said. Under the glare of the fluorescent ceiling light, his fair skin seemed pasty and his blonde hair looked dirty, although he had just washed it during his morning shower.

"Now, let's check her email. It was password

protected but we managed to open it up. It took awhile, but we got into it," the tech explained as he leaned over Zeek's shoulder and pointed to the icon for Outlook Express.

Clicking on the Outlook Express icon brought the email program onto the screen. About ten messages were in the inbox, all of which had been opened, but had not been erased.

"We hit the jackpot," the tech exclaimed beaming with satisfaction at their accomplishment in delivering the goods.

"Hey, you are right. There are some from Shiela, the other nuns, and Father Julian Parnell.

"Go ahead, be my guest, open them up!"

Zeek began opening the messages in the in-box one by one. He read an email from Shiela calling for a meeting of all the sisters after school the next day in the school library and a note from Sister Christa, asking Megan to lend her a certain book she needed for one of her classes.

"Look," the tech exclaimed excitedly, "Open that one from Father Julian. See, there it is! Look! Jparnell@landlink.net. It had been deleted, but we were able to retrieve it anyhow.

"Let's take a look at it," Rogers urged eagerly.

Clicking on the message that was dated about a week before she was killed, the following popped up on the screen: "I can't believe you are pregnant. I was very careful. You know I cannot marry you. You have known that all along. I am a priest and plan to remain one. I think you should have an abortion and the sooner the better. I'll be glad to pay for it."

The second email written two days later said the following:

"No, don't be ridiculous. You won't be killing our baby. It is just a fetus without all the elements of a human being. To proceed with the pregnancy would ruin both our lives. We had a good time, and we will have many more good times in the future. You know I really do care for you, but we need to get on with our lives now."

"We really did hit pay dirt!" Zeek exclaimed with a big smile on his face. "The priest was poking fun at her and got her knocked up. She wanted him to marry her and help her raise the kid. Looks like a good reason for murder. I'll get a warrant and arrest the bastard for murder one."

15
Christa

Fear hung over the convent ever since Sister Megan had been murdered. Christa found it very hard to believe that anyone could have killed her in cold blood right in the sacristy of Santiago. All the sisters were afraid, especially since Sister Shiela had channeled the horrible masculine entity into Sister Lotta. Sister Rose, the newest Ardorine to come to Santiago, was deathly afraid. In recent weeks, Christa noticed that Shiela had been sleeping frequently in Rose's room with her. Actually she was a bit jealous that the coordinator chose to sleep with Rose instead of her. Until Rose came to the convent, she had to share Shiela with Diane, but Shiela had taken turns in their beds and tried to be equitable in sharing her presence with them. Now Rose was monopolizing Shiela and enjoying her company almost every night. When she had mentioned it to Diane, she said that she resented Shiela's neglect and she had found other amusements to replace Shiela. When Christa asked Diane what her other amusements were, she received a very cryptic answer. "I take my delight East of the Sun and West of the Moon."

"What is that new crucifix that you are wearing, Christa?" Diane asked, as she picked it up off Christa's blouse and turned it around in the light so that she could get a better look at it.

"It is something I found on the internet and bought it. It is silver as you can see." She had just finished making her lesson plans for the coming week for the sixth grade.

"I have never seen anything like it, "Diane mumbled almost to herself as she sat down in the chair in Christa's room beside her study desk. "It looks like a naked woman on a cross! How strange!"

"It is of a woman on a cross being crucified. It is you and me and all the countless women in the Church down through the ages that have suffered repression because of the Old Boy Network. According to Thomas Aquinas a woman is a misbegotten male. Nature intends to make a male and something screws up the process and a female results—a misbegotten male."

"Yeah, I know," replied Diane. "Ever since Eve they have been blaming us for everything." She unbuttoned her slacks at the waist and took in a deep breath as she relaxed, without the wool slacks binding her so tightly.

"What's the trouble? Are you putting on a few pounds?" Christa asked as she saw what Diane had done.

"They are just a little tight. That's all." She glanced at her watch. "It is getting late. It is almost eleven and the clock alarm goes off early in the morning for school. I guess I had better go to my room now and turn in." Diane rose to leave.

"Since Shiela is sleeping with Rose almost every night, you can stay here with me if you want to," Christa invited with a smile.

"You probably won't believe this, but I really do have

a headache. Good night, Christa. You aren't afraid to sleep here by yourself, are you?" Diane asked lingering in the doorway of Christa's room.

"Yes, I am, now that you ask," Christa confided. I have been having terrible dreams at night. I actually dreamed of that Abraxas. He was holding me prisoner, and I awoke screaming, just as he was holding my head under water trying to drown me." Christa lowered her eyes and avoided looking at Diane.

"Really?" Diane asked. "I too have been having nightmares ever since Megan died and we had that awful channeling session when IX Chel vanished and Abraxas came and frightened us all." She thought a minute and added, "I'll go and get a couple of aspirin for my headache and my night gown and I'll be right back. I will spend the night in your room. If Abraxas shows up, we will fight him together," she said with determination.

16
Zeek

With a warrant for the arrest of Julian Parnell in hand, Zeek Zadek beckoned to Rogers, his partner, who had just entered their office at the Rosanada Police Headquarters, casually nibbling on a Danish and sipping a cup of Starbucks' black coffee.

"Hurry up, man, we got business to take care of. I got the warrant. Let's go."

"Ok, OK, I am ready, "Rogers answered as they headed for their steel gray Toyota patrol car parked in front of the station.

Because he was so anxious to make the arrest, Zeek turned the siren on in the car and lit up the cherry on the roof of the Toyota. With the siren wailing full blast, they sped up the river road to Santiago Church in the Gas'du Hills, hoping to reach the rectory, before Father Julian had a chance to leave for the day to go to his work at Catholic Charities.

As they approached Santiago, Zeek turned off the siren, so that they could pull up in front of the rectory quietly. Parking in front of the house, he and Officer Rogers made their way through the new fallen snow up the walk to the front door.

"Good morning, Valin," Zeek called out to Vogel who was busy shoveling snow from the walkway leading from the rectory to the church.

"Morning, Officers," Vogel returned his greeting as he continued his work.

When Zeek rang the door bell, it seemed like an interminable length of time before the black housekeeper finally answered.

"Yes, sir?" she asked with an intimidated look, as Zeek showed her his police badge.

"I want to see Father Julian Parnell? Is he here?" Zeek asked, carefully scrutinizing the woman's face.

"He is in the church, Sir. He will be back any minute to have his breakfast before he goes to Catholic Charities. You can come in and wait for him." She led them into the living room where Monsignor Petit was watching the morning news on the television.

"You wished to see me?" Monsignor Petit inquired a bit nervously.

"No, Reverend. We are waiting to see Father Julian Parnell." Zeek remarked casually, as he walked to the open fireplace and began to warm his hands that were quite chilled, because he had forgotten to wear his gloves. As they waited for Julian to return to the rectory, Rogers took a seat on the large brown sofa next to Monsignor Petit and settled down to watch the news. When the housekeeper appeared in the living room with a pot of coffee and some cups, Zeek eagerly poured himself a cup of the heady brew.

"Thank you, Ma'am. That was very kind of you," he said sincerely.

"We really do appreciate it, Ma'am," Rogers said as he poured his drink.

Sipping their coffee, they listened to news reports about thwarted terrorism attempts, pedophile priests, vandalism, and robberies in Rosanada. Within a few minutes Julian, who had apparently crossed from the church to the rectory through the subterranean passageways, since there was about a foot of snow on the ground, entered the living room.

"You wished to see me?" he inquired. He was dressed in a black clerical suit, had his car keys in hand, and appeared ready to leave for the day.

"Yes, we do." Without any preamble, Zeek came right to the point. "We are arresting you for the murder of Megan McGrath." He then proceeded to read him his rights. "Come with us," he ordered. "We are taking you into police headquarters where you will be able to phone your attorney.

In silence Julian got his overcoat from the closet by the entrance door to the rectory. Once he had the coat on, Zeek snapped handcuffs on his wrists and Rogers put the shackles on his legs. In utter silence, Julian walked with them to the patrol car.

17
Shiela

Ix Chel brought her peace. She was praying in the chapel for a few minutes before retiring for the night. Just when she was about to leave and go to her room—all the others had already left— Sister Diane came quietly to the chapel and sat down beside her. Diane Deladier—was a good friend and it was a real joy to have her as a member of the community. A very bright and pretty woman from Maine where her French Canadian ancestors had settled many years before, she was a bit of a health nut, loading up every day on such things as Vitamin E and fish oil, and even took an aspirin a day for her heart, not that she needed it, for she was in perfect health. However, she insisted that the reason she had good health was because of all the supplements she took. Outside of frequent headaches for which she took a lot of aspirin, she was in excellent health.

"Good evening, Diane," Shiela whispered as the petite young nun took her place on the cushions next to her.

"Good evening, I need to talk to you for a few minutes." Waiting to be told she could speak freely, Diane seemed to be experiencing anxiety, as she looked expectantly at Shiela. Because she was a strong woman and usually quite self-reliant, Shiela knew that something was weighing heavily on Diane, and she had come to her with a problem she could not work out by herself.

"What's wrong, Diane? You know you can tell me anything, and I will do my best to help you."

Running her fingers through her thick long black hair, Diane sighed deeply before continuing.

"I am pregnant, Shiela." Her blue eyes searched Shiela's to see what her response would be.

"Pregnant! Why weren't you more careful?" Shiela asked reproachfully. "There are way to prevent pregnancy and still have fun," she scolded. "How far along is your pregnancy?" Shiela asked as she eyed Diane carefully, trying to determine if the pregnancy was showing.

"I just found out. My period is overdue about four weeks and I bought one of those pregnancy tests at the drug store." She sighed deeply. "I am definitely pregnant." Diane seemed relieved now that she had told the coordinator her problem.

"It is easier to prevent pregnancy than to deal with it after the fact,"

Shiela said with annoyance creeping into her voice.

"Well, it happened. What do you suggest I do about it?" Diane asked on the verge of tears.

"Just calm down. The pregnancy has your emotions on edge. You will have an abortion, of course," Shiela said in a matter of fact tone. "We don't raise bastards like they used to do in congregations when nuns were indiscrete." She thought a few moments and added:

"It will be simple enough. I will use some of my discretionary funds to pay for it. No one need ever know anything about it. I will make the arrangements myself. At least we women now have the right to choose. After all we do have the right to decide what we do with our bodies." After pondering the situation a few seconds and staring intently into Diane's clear blue eyes, Shiela asked her: "Have you told the man who is responsible for your pregnancy?"

"No, of course not." Diane answered.

"Do you want to tell me who he is?"

"I would rather not." Diane fidgeted nervously with the buttons on her blouse.

"I understand. Perhaps that is for the best. If he knew, he might try to prevent your getting an abortion." Shiela folded her hands in a gesture of prayer and waited for Diane to tell her more.

"No, I don't want him to have any influence over me at all," Diane said adamantly. "I want to stay aloof—free—from him. We had fun together, but that is all that it was. Just a good time." She folded her hands in her lap and then looking up at Shiela said sadly: "It is always the woman who pays."

"Under those circumstances then you will return to your virginal state, because we know that virginity simply means that we keep free from male influence and domination. It is all right to enjoy sex as long as we do not get involved and we keep our minds and souls intact and free." She patted Diane's hand affectionately to show her support.

"Yes, Shiela, that is exactly the way I feel. We will just get rid of the tissues that are growing within me, and I will be myself again and be free again." She was relieved now that they were working for a solution.

"Don't worry, Diane, I will make all the arrangements and schedule the abortion and next week at this time you will be back to normal."

Shiela smile reassuringly, as Diane rose to her feet, nodded to Shiela and, bowing before the icon of Ix Chel, took leave of the chapel.

Shiela knew exactly how to handle Diane's problem. She herself had become pregnant last year and knew the clinic where she would send her. It would all be done very quietly. Realizing that many people would not understand about today's liberated nuns, the staff there was most discrete, and guaranteed absolute privacy and secrecy.

Early the next morning, Shiela phoned the clinic and spoke to Margaret Blackmore, the woman in charge, and was able to schedule the abortion for the following day when Dr. Kenneth Moreland would restore Megan to her virginal state.

When the morning came for Diane to go to the abortion clinic, Shiela helped her pack a small bag of things she might need just in case it were to become necessary for her to stay overnight, but she fully expected her to be back at Santiago convent a few hours after the out-patient surgery. It was such a simple procedure and very safe. A fresh pants suit, a nicely tailored one in navy blue, a few toilet articles, a shortie nightgown, a bra and panties, and plenty of pads for the bleeding all fit nicely into her blue overnight bag. As soon as the bag was packed, Shiela phoned a taxi, and sent Diane to the clinic.

When Diane returned later that afternoon, Shiela

helped her out of the taxi and carried her overnight bag into the convent, for she knew from her own personal experience that Diane was unable to carry anything. Although she had taken Percocet, a narcotic, to relieve the pain, Shiela could see that she was experiencing discomfort, as she walked painfully up the central staircase that led to the sisters' rooms on the second floor.

At dinner in the convent dining room, Shiela explained to the other sisters that Diane had not been feeling well and had seen a doctor and would be resting in her room for a couple days. If only Megan had followed her advice and had an abortion, perhaps she would still be alive, Shiela reasoned.

When they were just finishing dinner, the door chimes sounded, Shiela was delighted to see Teresa Valdés. It was wonderful how the laywomen always responded, when the sisters needed them. For the past year, Teresa had been coming to her for spiritual direction, and she had been able to help guide her in divorcing Antonio, her husband of twenty-five years. The woman suffered through a very disturbed childhood, having been the victim of incest for many years, with her father violating her repeatedly. As a consequence, she had become an alcoholic, spent time in rehabilitation in Alcoholics Anonymous, and finally now with Shiela's help and guidance had freed herself from an abusive husband and at last had peace in her life. Despite all the adverse things that she had experienced, Teresa Valdés was a handsome woman of about fifty that Shiela admired for her sense of style, since she was always dressed exquisitely in the latest fashions and her dark brown hair was always perfectly coiffed by Carlos at the same salon that Shiela visited every Saturday to have her own hair shampooed and set.

"I came to cheer you up a bit," Teresa said, as she handed Shiela an attractive basket of fruit, tied up with a large purple satin bow. Taking the gift, Shiela led her into the living room that was furnished with very modern Scandinavian furniture made of blonde woods and decorated with bold geometric prints.

"I can only stay a minute or two," Teresa continued as she took a seat on a lounge chair near the fireplace where a log was burning with small blue flames flickering over its surface.

Picking up a decanter of Scotch that graced the cocktail table in front of the sofa where Shiela was sitting, she said, "Let me pour you a drink, Teresa. I'll ring for some ice."

"No, thanks. I would rather have a cola."

"Of, course. I forgot. You don't drink. I'll get you one from the kitchen. Within a couple minutes Shiela returned with two cans of cola. Picking up two of the heavy crystal glasses that sat on the cocktail table, she poured the drinks and handed one to Teresa. "It is so nice of you to come, Teresa. I know we can always count on you for your prayers and support. We women simply must stick together."

"I can't help but think about Sister Megan and her tragic death. It is so sad. Such a lovely and dedicated young woman," Teresa said as she sipped her drink.

"Death is part of life, Teresa. We all have to go. Pain and suffering come to us all." Shiela noticed that Teresa seemed a bit unnerved from talking about death.

"Do you mind if I smoke?" Teresa was rummaging through her large red leather handbag that matched her shoes and completed her outfit—a striking red pants suit with a white blouse that ruffled around her neck.

"Of course not. I will smoke one with you."

Teresa pulled a gold cigarette case from her purse and extended it to her and lit her cigarette with the flame that sprang up when she spun the little wheel on her gold lighter.

"How are you doing now that your divorce is final?" Shiela asked, as she removed the jacket to her pants suit and placed it on the sofa beside her. The log in the fireplace was burning brighter now and the room was becoming very warm.

"I am fine. I feel like a new man." Teresa laughed softly.

"That is fine as long as you don't get entangled—keep your freedom. Have fun. Enjoy yourself, but guard your freedom," Shiela advised.

"I certainly will. Actually, I am seeing a man, but I will never marry again. I am taking your advice and am having a lot of fun," Teresa confided. Father Julian says it is all right for me to have sex with this man as long as we really care for each other." Teresa drew deeply on the long, filtered cigarette, drawing the smoke into her lungs and blowing it out her nose.

"Of course, Father Julian is very sympathetic and understanding of women and their problems.

He is not at all like old fashioned priests used to be. He also believes in homosexual marriage," Shiela explained.

"'I think they should be allowed to marry also," Teresa volunteered. She disposed of her cigarette by tossing it casually into the fireplace where the flames consumed it. Then rising to her feet, she said, "I really have to be going. I know this is a stressful time for all of you here in the convent. If there is anything I can do, please don't hesitate to phone me." She embraced Shiela and headed for the door.

After saying good night to Teresa and seeing her out, Shiela made her way up the central staircase to the second floor where she decided to look in on Diane to see how she was doing.

Since the house was very large, each one of the sisters had her own room with a bathroom *en suite.* After knocking gently on Diane's door so as not to awaken her, if she were sleeping, she turned the door knob and peaked into the room. She was relieved to see that Diane was propped up in bed wearing a pink satin bed jacket, reading a detective story.

"Mind if I come in for a few minutes?"

"Please do," Diane invited.

Shiela walked across the room to the very modern Swedish four poster bed and laid her hand on Diane's forehead.

"You seem a bit warm. Do you have a fever?"

"I do feel a bit hot and sometimes cold, but I think it will pass. It is probably just nerves acting up." Diane ran her petit slender hands through her long black hair.

Noting that her cheeks looked flushed and rosier than usual, contrasted with her fair complexion, Shiela said: "I'll get my thermometer and we will check your temperature to make sure." Quickly Shiela crossed the hall, entered her own room, retrieved her thermometer, returned to Diane's room, and put it into the nun's mouth.

In a few minutes Shiela examined the thermometer and announced, "You have a low grade fever. Shall I phone Dr. Moreland?"

"I hate to bother him at night. I'll just take a couple aspirin. Let's wait until morning and if it has not gone down, then we can call him."

"Are you in pain?" Shiela inquired solicitously.

"Yes, I have pain, but I am going to take the Percocet. It will stop the pain and put me to sleep in minutes. I am very sensitive to narcotics, but I am glad I have one tonight. I have a cramping feeling in my lower abdomen and some bleeding.

It is rather heavy, but they told me I would bleed for a while."

"I will get you a glass of water and the Percocet. Where is it?" Shiela asked trying to be helpful.

"The pills are here in the drawer in the bedside table," Diane said as she rummaged around in the drawer and found them and the aspirin, while Shiela got a glass of water in the bathroom and brought it to her.

After Diane swallowed the Percocet and the aspirin, Shiela bid her good night and retired to her own room where she listened to soft music on the radio to help her fall asleep. Before turning off the light, she picked up the statue of IX Chel that was on the table beside her bed and whispered a prayer to Goddess. Then, finally relaxed from the turmoil of the day, she fell into a deep sleep.

About five in the morning she awoke and decided to look in on Diane again to see how she was doing. After finding a flashlight in her closet, she put on her slippers and her white terry cloth robe, tiptoed across the hall to Diane's room, and carefully opened the door. Walking to Diane's bedside, she held her hand in front of the flashlight to shield the sleeping woman from the bright light, but had enough light to see how she was. Something did not seem quite right about Diane.

"Are you all right, Diane?" she asked pulling the sheet and the blanket down from her face. When Diane did not respond, she laid her hand on her face and repeated, "Are you all right, Diane?" Pulling back the bedding, she saw to her horror that Diane's nightgown was drenched in blood. She had lost an unbelievable amount of blood, and the bed was soaked in it.

"Wake up, Diane!" she called, taking her by the hand. When she did not stir at all, Shiela turned on the bedside lamp. Diane was very pale and her breathing was shallow. "Wake up!" she cried slapping her wrists briskly, but still unable to awaken her. The Percocet had stultified her, making her insensitive to her hemorrhaging. Seeing Diane's cell phone lying on the bedside table, she called 911.

"Send an ambulance to the convent at Santiago Church in the Gas'du Hills immediately," she cried in desperation.

When the ambulance arrived and the medics saw Diane's condition, they put her on a stretcher, wrapped her well in blankets, and took her out into the night to the waiting vehicle.

Climbing nimbly into the back of the ambulance, Shiela prayed fervently to Ix Chel who was celebrated for her solicitude for women and their female problems. "Ix Chel, come and help Diane who needs you very much."

However Ix Chel seemed far away and her prayers did not rise up out of the wailing ambulance, as it rushed to Divine Providence Hospital over the icy winter streets, while she was haunted by the insidious laughter of the one who called himself Abraxus and had mocked her, when she had channeled Lotta.

When Dr. Moreland, a very personable young surgeon, came into the emergency room to see Diane, he had a worried look on his face that told Shiela that he was deeply concerned about her loss of blood, her unconscious condition, and her labored breathing.

"She has lost an awful lot of blood," he said. "I am going to pack her and transfuse her, as soon as I can get the rare blood type that matches her needs," he explained as he took her pulse.

"Is she going to be all right," Shiela asked with great concern.

"I can't tell yet for sure. Her vital signs are poor. I don't understand why she is hemorrhaging so profusely. What medications is she taking beside the Percocet that I prescribed?" he asked taking his stethoscope in hand and proceeding to listen to her heart.

"She takes a lot of aspirin for headaches. She also took some before going to bed for the night because she had a low grade fever," Shiela replied.

"Anything else?"

"Just vitamins and some food supplements"

"Does she take Vitamin E and perhaps fish oil?"

"Why, yes she does as a matter of fact. How did you know?"

"They thin the blood and so does the aspirin and when a hemorrhage is caused by too much aspirin it is almost impossible to stop the bleeding. Why didn't she tell me she took these things before the surgery? She should have stopped them all two weeks before the procedure."

"She was anxious to get it over with," Shiela told him.

"That was a serious mistake," the doctor said shaking his head.

Shiela could see that Dr. Moreland was gravely concerned about Diane. Asking Shiela to go to the waiting room, he began working on Diane to try to stop the hemorrhaging.

As Shiela sat in the waiting room, she kept trying to pray to Ix Chel, but her prayers, she felt, were not being heard. After about two hours, nervously waiting for the doctor to advise her on Diane's condition, Dr. Moreland came to her.

"I have done everything I can for now. We will have her type blood later this morning. I sent for it and it is being flown in now. As soon as it gets here, we will give her a transfusion. Meanwhile, Sister, pray. Diane needs all the prayers she can get. She is in a much weakened condition. I suggest you contact her family and advise them to come at once." He folded his stethoscope and stuck it into the pocket of his white coat and sped down the hall, leaving Shiela in a state of bewilderment.

It was just breaking dawn when a taxi brought Christa

to the hospital to be with Diane, so that Shiela could return to the convent and the school. Once she was back home, Shiela phoned Diane's brother, her only living relative and advised him of the seriousness of Diane's condition.

When Shiela phoned Dr. Moreland later in the morning, his voice was heavy with sadness. "I have bad news for you. Diane is dying. I don't think she will last the hour. She has not regained consciousness. The hospital chaplain is with her. He is doing all he can. We all are. I am very sorry. Perhaps you will want to come at once?"

Deeply grieved over Diane's tragic situation, Shiela returned to the hospital and was with her when she breathed her last.

The darkness that hung over the convent intensified. All the sisters were aghast at the sorrowful turn of events. Even Sister Christa, who was usually optimistic and always looked on the bright side of things, was plunged into gloom as the specter of death seemed to be raging though the halls of Santiago.

18

Shiela

Phoning the motherhouse and informing Hilda that Diane was dead would be difficult. Waiting would not make it any easier, so she decided to get it over with, as soon as she could. She did not give her the details of Diane's surgery, but said simply that she had had surgery and the hemorrhaging was uncontrollable. When Hilda insisted on knowing the details of the tragedy, Shiela told her of the abortion. Mother Hilda received the news in silence, but insisted that they ship the body to Pennsylvania, where they would have her funeral. Unfortunately, however, she did not have another science teacher to send to replace Diane.

"Perhaps you can fill in for her and teach her classes, Shiela, since you majored in science and were a science teacher before you became principal.

"Of course, I will do that. Don't worry. We can manage. I won't be able to spend as much time in the office as principal, as I'd like, but I will manage."

"Perhaps Father Mel can find a lay teacher to fill in until the end of the year. May the angels protect you, Shiela. If you have any problems that I can help you with, don't hesitate to phone me. Good bye."

Shiela was concerned about how Christa would take the news of Diane's death. The two of them had been close. Actually Christa seemed to be recovering nicely from Megan's death and the unpleasant experience they had with channeling. Despite Mel's orders that they not do any more channeling at Santiago, Shiela was determined to have another channeling session soon. It was simply none of his damn business how they prayed, or what they did in their convent chapel. As far as she was concerned, Father Mel and his whole cockacratic establishment could just go to hell. Nuns were just zeros who worked like slaves without receiving any thanks or gratitude. So they had their inner migration. They had their own religion; like Joan of Arc, they embraced the craft and served the great mother Goddess. Since the parochial school children were entrusted to their care, they were learning about the Goddess too. In time woman power would rule the world like in the ancient matriarchal societies. Peace would come to humanity and a new golden age of spirituality would arise. She thought about how well Teresa Valdés and the other women of the parish were adapting to the things they were teaching them, enjoying being free of all the guilt and condemnation that the male priests put upon them. Why should men make decisions about pregnancy? What did they know about it? Why should they make any decisions at all about women's morality? She recalled the old saying about how men keep women barefoot in winter and pregnant in summer. With their morality, the priests sought to dominate women and keep them in subjection. Well, she was free and so were the rest of the women of the coven. She thought of Megan and Diane and of how their deaths had been caused by their involvement with men. There was a lot to be said in favor of lesbianism, Shiela reasoned, because a woman could not get pregnant, if she had her sex with another woman. As far as she personally was concerned, she could go either way. Actually she liked sleeping with Christa and Rose and some of the others. She also enjoyed Julian, but she would never get entangled with him, but would always keep aloof. However she was not prepared for what was about to take place.

19
Mel

Now that Father Julian had been arrested for the murder of Megan McGrath, he had been cleared of all charges. Life went on at Santiago, more or less, as usual. Julian's parents had immediately raised the bail for their only son, and he had returned to Santiago as soon as the judge had set bail. René Deladier, Diane's brother was suing Dr. Moreland for malpractice in the tragic death of his sister. Mel kept busy in the rectory office working on the accounts and paying the bills. A new shipment of sacramental wine had arrived, and he unpacked it and put it in the wine closet in the office. They were running low on wine, but still had a couple of bottles of the kind Father Julian used as well as several bottles of the wine he and Monsignor Petit preferred.

The daily routine was pretty much the same ever day. Father Julian had the Mass at 7:00, before he left for Catholic Charities, he had the 8:30, and Monsignor Petit always had the evening Mass at 7:00 pm. Since they usually met around the breakfast table each morning, they had a chance to catch up on what each was doing. This morning Mel was lingering over his second cup of coffee, reading the *Rosanada News*, and waiting for Father Julian to return from the church, hoping to catch him before he himself went to the church to celebrate his own Mass. There were some things he wanted to talk over with the young priest.

Glancing at his watch and noting that it was already ten after eight, he decided to head for the church and perhaps catch up with Father Julian in the sacristy. Since it was a very cold winter morning and Valin Vogel had not yet cleared all the snow from the walks, he decided to take the subterranean route to the church. Grabbing a flashlight he headed down the stairs from the pantry into the tunnels. When he emerged in the sacristy, he was filled with horror from what he saw. Father Julian was sprawled out on the floor almost in the same place that Megan was murdered. Still fully vested in a purple chasuble, he had apparently just finished saying Mass and putting the chalice on the cabinet, when he had collapsed on the floor. His face was flushed and quite pink with bluish tinges. Vomit stained the front on his chasuble with the smell of almonds clinging to him. He looked dead. Using the sacristy phone, Mel called 911.

"Send an ambulance to Santiago Church in the Gas'du Hills to the sacristy. Something is seriously wrong with one of the priests." Then as an after thought, he added, "Send the police too. It looks like an attempted murder, or murder."

Glancing through the sacristy door at the congregation, he saw that there were a handful of women waiting for him to say Mass. Too upset to celebrate Mass and with a priest sprawled unconscious on the sacristy floor under strange circumstance, he went into the sanctuary and announced solemnly:

"I am sorry. The Mass has been cancelled. I ask your prayers for Father Julian." Returning to the sacristy, he waited for the ambulance and the police to arrive, while observing Julian for signs of life. Seeing that he was still breathing, irregularly, but with short and shallow breaths, Mel hastened to the ambry to get the sacred oils. Fighting waves of nausea, he began anointing the priest's body and reciting the prayers for the dying.

When the ambulance arrived, the medics began examining Fr. Julian, commenting on the odor of almonds, the bright pink color of his face, the beads of perspiration on his forehead, and the blood tinged foam that oozed from his mouth. Soon the coroner, a tall black man in a black trench coat, arrived and placed a stethoscope to Julian's heart.

"Very irregular heart beat," he stated in a matter of fact manner."

The medics both nodded silently and one of them said:

"Judging from the looks of things and from the odor, I'd say it was potassium cyanide." Walking around Julian's body, as it lay sprawled on the oak floor of the sacristy, to the cabinet where Julian had placed his chalice, he commented unemotionally, "Probably drank poison from this cup." Without touching the chalice he bent over it and sniffed it, exclaiming, "Yup. It smells like bitter almonds."

Detective Zadek arrived within minutes, surveyed the situation carefully and directed his crew to photograph the crime scene and cordon off the area.

"Has anything been disturbed or removed?" He

glanced at Father Mel and then at the medics.

"I anointed him," Mel said.

"You did what?" asked Zadek, unfamiliar with Catholic practice.

"I gave him the last rites of the Church."

The medics had already bundled Julian up, placed him on a stretcher, and were in the process of carrying him to the ambulance. Noticing that there was a bit of the blood stained foam that had oozed from Julian's mouth on the sacristy floor, one of the medics laid a couple paper towels over the mess.

"Reverend, what can you tell me about all this?" Zadek asked, scowling at Mel.

"Not much I just came to the sacristy to get ready for my Mass at 8:30. Father Julian had Mass at 7:00. When I came into the sacristy about fifteen after eight, I found him like you saw him on the floor of the sacristy." Terribly shaken by what had happened to Julian, Mel had difficulty in expressing his thoughts.

"Well, you are pretty good at finding bodies in your sacristy," commented Zadek dryly. He directed his crew to secure the chalice that Julian had used to celebrate Mass and take it with them to the police van.

"He had wine in this cup?" Zadek asked as he began looking around the sacristy for the wine bottle from which Julian had partaken. "Where's the bottle of wine, Reverend?" he asked as he began opening and closing the doors of the cabinets.

"Right there," Mel said, pointing to a cabinet Zadek had not yet opened.

"Which one is it?" he asked, as he saw two different

wine bottles that were open in the cabinet.

"The darker one. It was his own. Monsignor Petit and I always use the other one."

Carefully so as not to obliterate any fingerprints, Zadek took the two opened bottles from the shelf and placed them in a plastic bag and handed them to one of his crew to take to the police van.

"Well, Reverend, they say lightening never strikes twice in the same place, but murder often does. I'll be leaving now, but I guarantee you, if that man dies, I will be back with a warrant in hand, charging you with murder one." The detective shrugged his shoulders and scowling at Mel, said: "Stay out of the crime scene. We want to investigate it more thoroughly."

Mel watched as the detective trudged through the snow to his police van, climbed in, and drove off. Numb, completely stunned by the horrendous turn of events, he was unable to pray, but keenly feeling the need for Divine guidance, he entered the church through the sacristy door and made his way to sit in front of the main altar, where he remained mute, pondering in his mind all that had happened.

When he finally returned to the rectory after about half an hour, he sought out Monsignor Petit and summoned him into the office to tell him what had happened. Petit, always in control of his emotions, replied to the grim story simply by saying very softly, "We better phone Catholic Charities and tell them Father Julian will not be at work today."

Mel nodded in agreement and sat stunned behind his office desk. Before he could reach for the phone,

Monsignor Petit asked, "Would you like me to phone them, Father?"

"Yes, please do. And call the emergency room at Divine Providence Hospital and see if there is any word on Father Julian's condition." Mel put his head down on his arms on his desk completely bewildered by all that had happened.

When Monsignor Petit finally got through to the emergency room at Divine Providence and explained who he was and why he was calling, he listened attentively. When he hung up the phone, he quietly related: "They say Julian is sinking fast.

He is convulsing and his heart beat is highly irregular and his breathing very slow and labored."

Within the hour Detectives Zadek and Rogers were ringing the doorbell at the rectory. Slowly Mel got up from his desk and facing the inevitable went to open the door.

"OK, Reverend," Zadek said flatly. "You know why we are here."

"We are arresting you for the murder of Julian Parnell," Rogers said, as he began to put handcuffs on Mel. "Better get your coat on first. It is very cold out there. While you are doing that, I will read you your rights."

Mel got his overcoat from the closet by the front door and then put his hands behind his back to receive the handcuffs. "We won't put the shackles on your legs, since you are willing to cooperate with us," Rogers said as he took Mel by the arm and led him out to the steel gray Toyota and pushed him roughly into the back seat.

When they arrived at the Rosanada Police headquarters, Mel was glad that they did not put him in a cell with other jail inmates, while they waited to book him. There would not be a recurrence of the brutal beating that he had suffered at the prior arrest.

When he was permitted to make his phone calls, he called Cristian Forte and arranged for him to represent him. With little hope of getting out on bail, he stretched out on the bunk bed in his cell and cried out to God for His protection and help.

20
Shiela

Julian's death was overwhelming. She did not realize how much he meant to her. Now that he was gone she felt a terrible emptiness come over her. Missing him more than she could possibly have imagined, she was consumed with pain—a horrible aching in her soul that nothing could assuage. His funeral had been unbearable. To bury their only son, his parents had flown home to Rosanada from the desert Southwest where they always wintered. The tolling of the funeral bell still echoed in her memory. With about ten priests concelebrating in the sanctuary of Santiago, Archbishop Hans Fuchs celebrated the Mass of the Resurrection for Father Julian, preaching a very eloquent homily in which he spoke of all the wonderful qualities of the young priest and of how his death was a great loss to the archdiocese. Because they all liked Julian and considered him a friend, all the nuns in the convent were in tears.

From his demeanor when he offered her and the Ardorines his sympathy on the death of Diane, as he greeted her after Julian's funeral, Shiela could sense that Bishop Del'Ano did not approve of her and her sisters. She had expected that, because Father Julian had told her that Bishop Del'Ano was very conservative. From what he had heard from various sources and related to her, she understood that the vicar general wanted to turn the clock back and return to the days before the Second Vatican Council. Furthermore, since her arrival in Rosanada, every time she had talked with him, she had sensed that he did not like women and had a basic, deep-rooted antipathy toward them. With his delicate and sensitive face, his slender, graceful hands, and effeminate mannerisms, it seemed obvious to her that he was gay.

Because Archbishop Fuchs supported them and was a good friend of Hilda, their provincial, she would not worry her head about Del'Ano. Recently, Hilda had forwarded to her and the other Ardorines at the Santiago convent, the lovely note Archbishop Fuchs had sent them all with his condolences upon the tragic death of Diane. Since the archbishop was a good friend, it really did not matter what Del'Ano with his antiquarian beliefs thought about them.

Nevertheless, it was really regrettable that the channeling session had turned out so miserably.

How much she had wanted to bring Ix Chel to the sisters who really needed the consolation of the Goddess, when Megan was killed. Lotta must have been suffering from some childhood trauma that caused the disturbance. At least that is how Julian had explained it to her. In spite of Father Mel's adamant demand that they refrain from channeling, she would simply have to try channeling IX Chel again soon. She certainly wasn't going to let him come between her and the Goddess.

Since the police were finished investigating Megan's

room, Christa helped Rose pack up all the dead woman's things and put them in boxes and carry them to the attic so that Rose could move in. Although the hard drive of Megan's computer had been returned to the convent, the police had made a backup copy of all that was on it, before reformatting the disk. Obviously they had found something on it that made it possible for them to arrest Julian for her murder, but because Julian had also been murdered they did not release that information.

Shiela was glad that Sister Lottta seemed to have suffered no ill effects as a result of the channeling session that turned out badly. In fact, Lotta was begging her to put her in touch with the supernatural again soon.

21
Zeek

Although he had been absolutely certain that Julian Parnell killed Megan McGrath, he had to rethink the entire case, now that Julian himself had been murdered. Shannon had to be the guilty party. No doubt he had killed both the McGrath woman and Julian Parnell, but he still had a few more leads that he had to check out.

Motioning to Rogers to hurry up, he said, "Let's go. I got the warrant to search Julian Parnell's family home, his office, and his computer at Catholic Charities. We will go there first to get the computer hard drive and then go to the Parnell house. I think his parents are in residence there, since they returned for the funeral." Driving more slowly than usual because of the clumps of thick black ice that had accumulated in the city streets, they went down the river road to the Catholic Charities building that was situated next to the Rosanada Chancery Offices.

"It looks like we are in for more snow," Rogers said as he bent over and craned his neck to look up at the heavily clouded sky.

"Well, that is to be expected now that December is here. Won't be long now 'til Hanukah," Zeek replied. "Margie and I always go to my folks for Hanukah. My mom always has a big dinner celebration, perhaps you and your wife might join us. I am sure Mom will be happy to set a couple extra places at the table."

"That is real nice of you, Zeek, to invite us. I'll tell Jill about it," he said referring to his wife of fifteen years.

At Catholic Charities, they were led into Julian's office by the receptionist, when Rogers flashed his police badge and the search warrant. Quickly they went through the drawers in Julian's desk and found nothing but case studies of the people he had been assigned to work with. There was nothing in the closet either, except a couple old sweaters, a Notre Dame jacket, and a smelly pair of sneakers. Perhaps the computer would afford them some valuable information that would help them assemble some of the missing pieces of the puzzle of Megan McGrath's and Parnell's deaths.

Snow was beginning to fall when they dropped the computer hard drive off with the technicians at police headquarters. Thick swirling flakes made it difficult to see, as they proceeded to the Parnell home.

When they parked under the porte-cochère of the Parnell home, the day had become dark and ominous with a blizzard moving in. Tall pillars decorated with Corinthian capitals stood like sentinels in front of the expansive Georgian style brick home that looked to be about ninety years old. Zadek had head that the Parnells had made their money in lumber many years before and that Julian's father had been retired ever since he turned thirty years of age. Although he studied to be an attorney and had successfully passed the bar exam, he never practiced law.

A maid in a black dress and white ruffled apron

answered the door and looked at them in alarm, when they showed her their police badges.

"We have a search warrant, Ma'am," Zadek said politely. "May we come in?"

"Wait, I will get Mr. Parnell," she said and retreated into the darkness of the house, closing the door in their faces.

A few minutes later, a mature man pulled open the heavy oak door that bore the initials JJP etched in a heavy plate glass pane and peered cautiously out at them. Impeccably dressed in a gray wool sweater and gray flannel slacks, he looked like he had just stepped from the pages of a man's fashion magazine. Zeek figured he was about sixty, as he studied his bald head that sported a fringe of gray hair above the ears and at the base of his skull.

"Yes? What can I do for you," he asked coldly, but civilly, holding the door open about half way.

"Sorry to bother you, Sir, at this time. We are sorry for your loss and offer our condolences. Your son has been brutally murdered and we are determined to find the killer," Zadek explained patiently.

"Who is there, dear?" a woman's voice called from somewhere in an adjoining room as they entered the house and were waiting for Parnell to hear what they had to say. When a woman of about sixty joined them, they assumed that she was Julian's mother. A small woman with gracious features, she was dressed fashionably in a dark blue suit. "These gentlemen are from the police. This is uh… I don't believe I got your names." Parnell said, as he motioned for them to come into the living room and be seated.

"Sorry, I'm Detective Zadek and this is my partner Detective Rogers."

"Thank God you have come. We will do everything we can to help you find out who killed our son," Parnell said flatly as he put his arm around the shoulders of his wife who was beginning to cry.

Zadek could see that Mrs. Parnell was deeply grief stricken, as she daubed her eyes with a tissue and sniffled.

"We have a warrant to search the premises. We are especially interested in searching your son's room and his personal effects. Would you lead us there, please?" Rogers asked, as he waited for the Parnells to show them the way.

Interestingly, they had a large living room on either side of the entrance hall. One room was furnished in green overstuffed furniture and had massive oak book cases flanking the wall opposite a fireplace that was boasting a large oak log that flamed brightly. On the ceiling around the perimeter of the room were paintings of the American presidents and the various American flags, as they existed in the different times down though the history of the presidencies of the men depicted. The most recent flag had forty-eight stars. The other living room was decorated in pink with flowers and ribbons painted on the ceiling. Heavy brocaded draperies hung at the windows.

As they began following Joseph Parnell up the massive central stairway, Zadek slipped off his coat and unbuttoned his bulky brown sweater. The house was very warm, and he figured the Parnells must have set the thermostat on eighty degrees and had an enormous heating bill.

"I guess you find the house awfully warm," Parnell said when he saw Zeek take off his coat and unbutton his sweater. "We just got back from Arizona and we are not used to the cold," Parnell explained.

As they reached the landing on the staircase, Rogers began to admire the stained glass window he saw there in which a stag was drinking from a mountain stream. "They don't make houses like this any more," he commented dryly.

"The house was built by my father many years ago."

When they reached the top of the stairs, Parnell, pointing at a room that lay straight ahead said: "That is Julian's room. Go ahead, Detectives, and do what you have to do." Parnell entered the room, followed by Zadek and Rogers, and took a seat in a recliner in front of the fireplace. Mrs. Parnell had disappeared somewhere into another room on the second floor. Because the room was not occupied since Julian's death, there was no fire burning in the fireplace.

Surveying the room, Rogers noted a highboy dresser and began to go through the contents of the drawers, while Zadek headed for the clothes closet and began sorting through Julian suits and sports jackets. It was a large walk-in closet where Julian kept his golf clubs—a complete set of matched irons and woods. There was also a tennis racquet, bowling shoes, a large bow and a quiver full of arrows, skis, and even a pair of ice skates. Obviously, Zadek decided, Julian was definitely the athletic type.

Approaching Julian's roll top desk next to the large casement window overlooking the porte-cochère, Zadek began looking at the personal computer that sat on it.

"Sir," Zadek said to Parnell who was watching his every move, "we will have to take the computer hard drive with us to police headquarters. It may contain information that will help us find your son's killer."

"Of course, Officer, you are welcome to it, if it will be of any help to you."

Adroitly, Zadek took the case off Julian's computer and Rogers retrieved the hard drive and put it in a plastic envelope and stuck it in the pocket of his trench coat. "Now show us the top two floors," Zadek requested.

"All right. We have bedrooms on the third floor and a ball room on the fourth. Come, I will show you," Parnell offered. Zeek could see that the man was painfully grief stricken over the death of his son. Deep furrows etched his cheeks and a tear seemed to glisten in his gray eyes.

Quickly Zadek and Rogers toured the upper two floors of the house, but found nothing of further interest After thanking the Parnells for their help, they sped away to take the two hard drives Julian had used to the computer lab for analysis, hoping to get the results back quickly, because a murderer was at large and could strike again at any moment.

22

Mel

In spite of the fact that Detective Zadek said he would not get bail, Cristian Forte and Monsignor Petit managed to get him out of jail after only three days. Mel was sure that Archbishop Fuchs had used his influence with the judge to accomplish this. Even though he had been gone from the parish for just a short time, work had piled up high on his desk. Monsignor Petit kept asking him to cancel the special service the Sisters of the Holy Ardor were planning for the following week.

"I told Sister Shiela that I was going to cancel their women's service. With Julian dead and not participating in it as planned, I thought it would be easy to cancel it. But no! She insists on going through with it. She says they do not need a priest that *she* will minister to the women. "Monsignor Petit shook his head sadly and sighed deeply. "To be perfectly frank, I wish we could get rid of the Ardorines." His gray eyes were troubled and a deep frown creased his brow. He rubbed his nose, a gesture that always reflected his concern and worry.

"I understand how you feel, Monsignor. I will talk to Sister Shiela and to Bishop Del'Ano again about them.

"Are you planning to go to the school to see her?"

"No, I will meet with her on my turf, not hers. I'll

phone the school and set up an appointment with her secretary to meet with her here."

No sooner said than done, and he had it all arranged with Jean Wilson for Shiela to come to the rectory at four that afternoon.

Promptly at four o'clock, Shiela rang the door bell and waited for Nirvana to let her in.

"Go right in, Sistah," Nivarva said as she ushered Shiela into the house, took her heavy faux fur coat, shook the snow off it, and hung it in the closet. Carefully Shiela kicked the damp snow from her boots, and taking off her red wool hat and scarf to match, handed them to Nirvana to put in the closet.

"Come in, Sister Shiela," Mel said as he stood in the doorway of the rectory office, motioning to her to take a chair.

Sitting down in the gray leather chair across from his desk. Shiela crossed her legs, careful not to muss her bright red pants suit.

"You wanted to see me?" she asked with her left eyebrow arched imperiously.

"Yes, there are a few things that I want to discuss with you." He paused and watched her as she sat primly waiting to hear what was on his mind.

"I am planning to cancel the day long retreat you have scheduled for the women of the parish for Saturday of next week." Carefully observing her reaction to his words, he continued, "I am going to put the cancellation notice in the church bulletin this Sunday."

Taking a deep breath and sitting up taller in her chair, Shiela asked abrasively, "Why, pray tell, have you decided to do that?"

"I am doing it because I am responsible for the souls of the people in my care here at Santiago. I am opposed to your prayers that you begin saying: 'In the name of the Creator, Redeemer, and Sanctifier.'

That is not the way the Church prays and has prayed for about two thousand years. Your prayer, "Our Mother, who art in heaven" is also totally unacceptable. That is not the Lord's prayer—he taught us to pray saying, 'Our Father who art in heaven.'"

He could see that Shiela's face was turning red with flaming anger boiling up within her.

"I am opposed to your constant references to the Holy Spirit as 'she.' Furthermore we do not worship someone called Sophia—or for that matter, any other goddess.

"But I …" She tried to speak, but he cut her off.

"I am not finished, Sister. Several times recently one of your sisters has used white-out on the lectionary and written in inclusive language. Need I remind you that is against canon law?"

When she tried again to speak, he told her, "I am not finished yet."

He could see that her knuckles on both hands were white, as she clutched tightly to the arms of her chair.

"I want you to know," he continued "that I discussed your channeling episode at length with the vicar general. Bishop Del'Ano is very much opposed to channeling and told me that he would take up the matter with Archbishop Fuchs. You are skating on thin ice, Sister. You better mend your ways and your liturgies or you and the rest of the Ardorines will be leaving the Rosanada Archdiocese." He eyed her coolly and said, "Ok. You may talk now."

With complete self-assurance, Shiela told him in no uncertain terms: "Archbishop Fuchs is a very good friend of Mother Hilda, our provincial. We just received a lovely note of condolence from him the other day in which he said he hoped our tenure in Rosanada would be long. I think rather that it is you who might not have a long time to remain in Rosanada, according to Detective Zadek."

Mel winced at the mention of Zadek, recalling that he had charged him with the murder of Father Julian. Glaring at her, Mel rose to his feet and said coolly, "Thank you for coming. Good day! I will get your coat for you."

Handing Shiela her back faux mink coat and her hat and scarf, he walked her to the door. As she turned from him and started to leave, he could hear her mumble "Son of a bitch! Cockacratic bastard!" Then looking at him over her shoulder, she said with teeth clenched,

"You have not heard the last of this!"

"Nor have you," he countered back.

23

Monsignor Petit

Although the confirmation was scheduled for the tenth of December, Monsignor Petit did not consider the young people ready to receive the awesome sacrament. The Ardorines were simply not teaching them the faith. He had asked one young man why God had created him and got the response, "She made me to know her in this life and gradually to return to oneness with her in eternity." "*C'était incroyable*!" Perhaps, he reasoned, if Bishop Del'Ano just took the time to questions some of the kids to be confirmed, he would understand better what the Ardorines were doing in the school, or rather what they were failing to do. He never thought the educational system would fall so short of what it should be. Why the sisters even brought the children to their first communion without their having gone to first confession! When he asked the children about their sins, they all cried out, "We don't have any sins!" "*Incroyable*!" He had asked one of the first communicants what it is was that they were going to receive and was told. "Sister said it is just a wafer—it is just a symbol."

When he asked one of the teenage boys about what confirmation meant, the young man said, "She who is will bless me with many gifts and make me open to enlightenment." Another boy in the confirmation class told him that sacraments are communion with nature and the Mass is a cosmic celebration of the community. Another one told him that priesthood is a common bond of all creatures, that angels are spiritual creatures in charge of guiding us, and that Jesus is an emanation of the divinity. "*C'était incroyable*!" He shook his head in utter dismay.

The dark days of December seemed even darker with the deaths of the two nuns and Father Julian. Although the young priest had been very liberal and did not seem to believe in the supernatural dimensions of the faith, he was a likeable fellow, and he missed his smiling face and optimistic conversation at the dinner table. He felt sorry for Julian's parents. They would not have much joy this Christmas. When he had seen them at the Sunday Mass, they were both deeply enveloped in their grief. He had shaken their hands as they filed out of church and tried to say a few words of consolation to them, but what can you say to an aging couple whose only son has been senselessly murdered?

24
Shiela

Still furious the next day after her conversation with Mel, Shiela decided to defy him and hold a channeling session. She'd be damned if she would pay attention to his order to desist from bringing Ix Chel to the coven! She was worn out and depressed. They all were. Teaching Diane's classes and doing her own work as principal was a heavy load. They had tried to find a laywoman to take over the science classes, but so far had no success. What they all needed now were the tender ministrations of Ix Chel, speaking through Sister Lotta.

To assemble the sisters in the chapel that night after dinner, she announced her intention to channel Lotta over the intercom that went into each sister's room. Going to the chapel and kneeling in prayer, imploring the Goddess to be with them, she waited for the sisters to assemble. There were only eleven of them now, because Diane wouldn't be replaced until the next class graduated from college in the Spring.

Lotta was eager to go ahead with the channeling. Dancing blithely inside the circle of nuns, Shiela set the circle as she sprinkled each of the sisters with a holly branch dipped in holy water that she herself had blessed in the name of the Goddess. Red candles were ablaze on the altar at the foot of the grand icon of Ix Chel.

Taking her place at her harp placed next to the altar, Lotta suggested: "Let us begin by singing 'Ix Chel, fair maiden, gentle mother and most wise crone." Shiela loved to hear Lotta play the beautiful stringed music that was so comforting and soothing to a tired spirit. Blending melodiously, the sisters voices joined in the hymn of praise. Immediately when they finished the song, Shiela introduced another song, and then another and another until the entire coven was relaxed and at peace.

"Come, Lotta," Shiela invited motioning for her to come and kneel on a cushion before her. Lotta did as she was bidden to do. Soon she began to rock slowly from side to side with her eyes closed and a happy smile on her face. Ix Chel was near now. Shiela could tell that from the expression on Lotta's face, because they had experienced the presence of the Goddess many times together. Laying her hand lightly on Lotta's shoulder, she said, "Welcome, Ix Chel, come to us. We need you. We are weary and wounded and need your gentle touch and energy."

"*Alieschamoo! Alieschamoo*!" the sisters murmured in a strange unknown tongue. "Yes, speak to us," Christa pleaded with tears in her eyes, because she missed Diane so very much.

Eyes closed tightly and her body held in a rigid position, as she knelt on the cushion before Shiela, Lotta began to speak very softly at first, and then her voice began to rise slowly, until everyone in the chapel could hear her. "I am she who is—she who is—darkness is gone, I come in light to bring you into the spiritual realm and bless you, my daughters."

With deep attention the sisters all drew closer to Lotta and began questioning her.

"How can we be guided in peace?" little Sister Rose asked timidly.

"Be loving and kind to each other," Ix Chel said in a musical voice that sounded very different from Lotta's usual husky tones.

"And Father Julian?" Shiela asked boldly. "Is he ascending?"

"He is with the Sun God. He too is happy," Ix Chel assured them through Lotta. Continuing she said, "Now, Sisters, I, Ix Chel, want you to dance and be happy and love one another. Play the organ, Shiela, and let everyone dance and be happy." Shiela rose to her feet and proceeded to the organ as Ix Chel had bidden her to do and began playing it—something she only did on special feast days. Softly she played *Liebestraum*, followed by Beethoven's *Moonlight Sonata* and then some Tchaikovsky and Grieg.

"Play Christmas carols, Shiela," one of the nuns begged. The rest of them took up her request so she began playing "Jingle Bells" and other songs like "Rudolph the Red Nosed Reindeer" and "Frosty the Snowman." She did not mind playing the secular music of Christmas, but she was not about to play hymns to the male child in the manger.

Glancing over at Lotta, she noticed that she had fallen back on the cushions and was sleeping soundly with a smile on her face.

With a full heart, Shiela thanked Ix Chel for coming to them and blessing them. All the sisters were happy, as they sat in a circle around her, holding hands, and singing, as she played the songs they wanted to hear. She too was happy. They were the first moments of peace and happiness she had known since Julian's death. As the sisters began to leave the chapel. Shiela motioned to Christa to come and sit beside her. When the others had all left, Shiela rose to her feet, slipped gracefully over to the altar, skipping from one stepping stone to the next. Blowing out the candles and bowing before the icon of Ix Chel, she motioned to Christa to come and join her as she left the chapel. Arm in arm they climbed the stairs to the second floor. Christa was radiant as Shiela took her by the hand and drew her into her room. "Come, Little One, and spend the night in my bed," she said as she began unbuttoning Christa's blouse.

25
Bishop Del'Ano

For the first time in his life, Renato was happy, profoundly happy. After the troubling years of Archbishop L'Abbadon's tenure in Rosanada, he had finally found peace and contentment living with John Bugumil in Casa St. Popola. They had the entire top floor of the house to themselves and Renato rejoiced that Archbishop Fuchs understood about same sex relationships and accepted them. No dark clouds were on the horizon, and he was even considering making a trip back to Torricella to see his aging mother, but he just had not had the time to do it. As vicar general, his presence was required in Rosanada, but he managed to send her money every month, grateful to her that she had believed in him when no one else did. She always knew that he would become a good priest. He would liked to have visited his old friends at the Shepherds of the Lord in Rome too. They also had believed in him and made it possible for him to be where he was now.

John Bugumil was the best companion he had ever found. They both laughed together about how John was known in the archdiocese as "Vlad, the Impaler" in the days before he was consecrated a bishop. In their life together, they had settled down to a very comfortable routine. Because they both had served as L'Abbadon's secretaries and had lived with him and catered to his every desire, they had something in common on which they could build a relationship.

They also laughed often about how L'Abbadon had referred to John as "Mr. Bug" and about how when either of them made him Canadian Club Manhattans, the old archbishop would not let them drink any of them. Finding it hilarious, John laughed heartily when Renato told him how he had made Manhattans and put olives in them instead of cherries. When he demonstrated how the old archbishop had pitched a tantrum by stamping his feet and shouting because of the cherries, they both were in stitches. They made a good pair. John was big and muscular and very masculine while he, Renato, had a slight build and soft gentle features, and slender tapering fingers.

After his morning appointment, Renato had rushed home to Casa St. Popola to get dressed to go with Hans Fuchs to a leisurely business lunch. He picked out his finest linen shirt with French cuffs and selected his most ostentatious cuff links—heavy gold ones studded with emeralds that he had bought since his investments were flourishing. Donning his best Italian tailored clerical suit that he had bought in Rome when he accompanied Hans on his *ad limina* visit to see the pope, he carefully placed around his neck the chain of the ornate gold pectoral cross that his mother gave him when he was consecrated a bishop and placed the cross itself inside the breast pocket of his jacket.

"How do I look, Mr. Bug?" he asked Bugumil who

was watching him dress.

"Very handsome, Renato," John replied.

Looking in the full length mirror on the door of his bedroom, Renato decided that he did look great. German born and bred, Hans was a stickler for formalities and always dressed in expensive hand tailored suits and expected Renato to do the same.

Since Hans was sending his limo to pick him up promptly at one, he was ready ten minutes earlier and went to wait for him in the living room on the first floor. He did not like to spend much time there, because Bishop Rivera who was suffering from dementia was always there and would try to strike up a conversation with him. It never failed to happen.

"Good evening, Bishop Rivera," he greeted the old fellow who was wearing a faded pair of blue jeans. In his hand he had his episcopal croisier that he kept banging up and down on the floor of the living room for emphasis as he spoke.

"You may kiss my ring," Bishop Rivera said extending his hand.

In a perfunctory manner, just to placate the demented bishop, Renato picked up his hand and pressed his ring casually to his lips.

"No! No! That is not how you do it," he protested. "You must bend over and bow when you kiss my ring, Stamping both feet, the old bishop turned his back on Renato and walked away mumbling to himself.

To avoid any further encounters with Bishop Rivera or the other demented tenants of Casa St. Popola, Renato decided to wait outside in front of the house, even though a winter chill was in the air. Hoping that Hans would take him to Chez Georges, a delightful French restaurant, where the archbishop kept an open tab and often wined and dined people at the archdiocesan expense, Renato looked forward with much anticipation to the business lunch with Hans, especially since he always enjoyed French cuisine.

When promptly at one Fritz, the archbishop's servant dressed in very fashionable blue livery, pulled up in front of St. Popola's in the archbishop's long black limo, Renato casually waited while he got out of the vehicle, came around to where he was standing, opened the door of the vehicle, and greeted him formally, as he stood tall and straight. "*Guten Tag, Herr Bischof!*"

"Good day, Fritz," he returned the greeting.

Comfortably ensconced and awaiting his arrival, Hans Fuchs was already in the limo.

"Hop in, Renato, I know this delightful Morrocan Arab restaurant overlooking the Rosanada River where I often go for business lunches. I thought you would enjoy it. I don't think I have ever taken you there before. They have the most delicious lamb. I have always enjoyed Arab restaurants; I used to go to one in Vienna that was fantastic." A stickler for formalities, he shook Renato's hand, as he welcomed him into the limo.

Although he detested lamb, Renato smiled and thanked Hans for taking him to such an interesting restaurant. Actually he had never before visited an Arab restaurant. It turned out to be more than he had bargained for.

When Fritz dropped them off on the red carpet that

lined the walkway under a long black canopy leading to the entrance of Al Amir, a doorman in a handsome black uniform greeted them.

"Good day, Archbishop, welcome to Al Amir," he said bowing before the prelate. "Your Excellency is most welcome."

"Good day to you, Yusef."

No sooner were they inside the door of the restaurant when the *maître d*, a tall dark man, obviously an Arab, dressed in formal attire and wearing tails, began fluttering around them.

"Good afternoon, Your Excellency, I'll show you to your usual place. After picking up a couple of large, gaudy gold menus from a table that stood nearby, he began leading them through the darkened dining room to a salon privé in the back of the establishment.

In the private room, two waiters, both dressed in tuxedos, were putting the last touches on the table that was only about eighteen inches off the floor. A vase of white orchids in the middle of the table caught Renato's eye as his waiter—they each had their own personal waiter and his was Ali—invited him to sit down on the cushions surrounding the table.

As Hans sat down across the table from him, leaning back on the plush purple cushions, he greeted the waiters by name and then began perusing the voluminous menu that the *maître d'* handed him. When Renato glanced at his menu, he was unable to fathom the Arabic names. Since he simply could not identify with any of the foods, he would just have to ask Hans to order for them both.

When the wine steward came to their table, he greeted

the archbishop cordially and inquired: "Shall I bring you your favorite, Your Excellency?"

"Yes, of course, the Dom Perignon 1990 Oenothèque will be fine, Hadad." Then to Renato he said, "You will like this wine. It is very rich, almost creamy, but at the same time elegant and very tasty."

After looking at the menu carefully for several minutes, Hans asked: "Well, are you ready to order, Renato? Everything is excellent."

"Please order for both of us, Renato said, "You are familiar with what they have here. I'll trust your judgment, Hans."

"What do you recommend for the *mezza*, Abdul?" the archbishop asked.

"The *magdoos* are excellent today and so is he *bamieh*."

"Good, we will have some of each and some of the *maanik*. For salad, bring us each *fatoosh*."

As Hans continued with ordering the meal, Renato gazed around their private dining room, amazed that it was so large for just the two of them, since it was about twenty feet square. Lavish red and purple hangings containing fiber optic lighting decorated the walls. On one end of the room a platform was raised about six inches above the floor that was carpeted in thick Turkish carpet decorated with geometric designs.

When the wine steward came with the Dom Perignon and poured it in their glasses, the purple hangings behind the platform opened up and three men that were dressed in white kaftans and each sporting a red fez with a black tassel entered the room, taking seats on some folding chairs that were lying on the floor of the platform. To

Renato, they looked like the terrorists he had seen on television.

"*Ach so*!" Hans exclaimed with enthusiasm. "Our musicians have arrived. Now you are in for a treat, Renato. Look, see the long flute the man on the left is holding—that is a *khallool*—one of the oldest wind instruments in the world. The chap in the middle, the short fat man, he is getting ready to play his *hajouje*. It's a wooden bass instrument from North Africa. The other chap has a *bender*—it is a small goatskin-covered wooden drum." The archbishop smiled contentedly as he sipped his champagne and listened to the strange exotic music that the trio was making. It was like nothing Renato had ever heard before with the haunting tones of the flute, the jangling sounds of the hajouje, and the incessant pounding of the *bender*.

When Ali started setting the *mezza* in front of him, Renato tasted it carefully, uncertain as to what it was and if he would like it. After taking a few bites, he decided the *magdoos* were not for him. The *bamieh* wasn't any better; it was seasoned with cilantro which he simply could not stand. The *maanik* turned out to be some kind of sausage and he had managed to eat a few mouthfuls when the *fatoosh* arrived. Finally they had brought him something he could eat—it was a tomato and cucumber salad. As he munched on his salad, he thought about the things he wanted to discuss with Hans at this business lunch. So far there had been no opportunity to talk. Just as he was ready to broach the subject of the Ardorines, hoping to get them driven from the archdiocese, the hangings behind the platform opened again and three women dressed flamboyantly in seductive Oriental dance costumes entered and began spinning around the room. They were all three wearing translucent purple skirts that hugged their hips about four inches below the waist, revealing their bare navels and midriffs, as they danced with bare feet, swaying sensuously to the music. Clinging to their ample breasts, they wore brief tops that left the rest of their torsos naked, except for the elaborate necklaces of coins that jangled with every step they took, as they undulated to the exotic Arabic music. Long dangling earrings swung from beneath their luxuriant black flowing hair that was polished like marble and sparkled in the mysterious light of the fiber optics hidden in the wall hangings.

Renato could not believe his eyes as one of them danced up to him and began flirting with him boldly as she wiggled and shook her ample hips. When she danced away, another one came up and danced right beside him, gyrating and spinning as she jiggled her hips with strange little pelvic thrusts. They reminded him of the cheap hoochie koochie dancers that came to Torricella with the traveling fairs when he was a boy. His disgust must have shown on his face, for Hans began defending the dancers.

"Belly dancing is a great art form," Hans explained expansively. "It has a long and great cultural heritage. Actually, It is one of the oldest of all art forms. Women invented it to use in worship of the Great Mother Goddess. In France, I saw a bas-relief called the Venus of Laussel. It was found in a cave in the Dordogne Valley and they estimate it goes back to about 19,000 years before the Common Era. It is the oldest example of Mother dancing that exits. However, there are many depictions of women dancing with their arms upraised in the Stone Age caves of Europe."

Renato was still not impressed with the gyrations of the female body that he was forced to observe. He simply could not believe that his archbishop had brought him to such a place. At any minute he fully expected a whirling dervish to appear.

When the dance was finished, the girls and musicians left to go to perform for other customers, but Abdul assured the archbishop that they would return later to dance and play again.

"And now for the *pièce de resistance*," exclaimed Abdul as he and Ali disappeared into the hangings that decorated the back wall of the room. Returning almost instantly, each one had in his hands a long scimitar about four feet in length that he held high over his head. The scimitars were laden with pieces of meat, potatoes, carrots, and whole tomatoes—all sizzling hot on the blazing swords that pierced them. Renato watched as Ali began taking the meat from his sword and placing it on a large plate in front of him. The smell of the meat and vegetables was very tantalizing for Renato as he waited to try them.

Hans was already eating his and encouraging him to enjoy the meal. As he took a bite-sized morsel of meat into his mouth and tasted it, he discovered that it was lamb, and not beef as he had hoped. Although he detested lamb and its strong flavor, he chewed it up and forced it down with a big gulp of the Perignon.

Because he had some concerns on his mind, Renato decided to broach the subject that most troubled him, and they could talk in peace, before the belly dancers and the musicians returned with all their noise and confusion.

"I wanted to talk to you about the Ardorines," he ventured as he leaned back on the thick, purple cushions and carefully observed the archbishop's reactions to what he said. Renato figured that the food and the music had probably put the archbishop in a pleasant mood, and it would be a good time to talk to him.

"Fine group of women," Hans replied. "We are lucky to get them. Sisters are hard to get these days. Almost impossible. The only reason we got them is because I am good friends with Brunhilda, their mother provincial up in Pennsylvania."

Renato could see that Hans was enjoying his lunch very much as he cut off a large piece of lamb and put it in his mouth. Since the archbishop seemed so favorably disposed toward the Ardorines, Renato sensed that he would have to proceed very carefully with anything he might say about them.

"Yes, fine women," he replied. "Well educated with excellent teaching credentials." He hesitated before coming to the point he wished to discuss.

"What is on your mind exactly," the archbishop asked as sipped his French champagne.

"There was a strange episode recently at the convent," Renato told him, realizing that he would have to tell the archbishop exactly what had occurred with Lotta Biermann.

"Yes? What happened?"

"They were channeling."

"That is a fad these days. Lots of people are into it. I can't see any harm in it," Hans said as he continued avidly eating.

"Well, Hans, it got out of hand somehow," Renato stated as a preliminary to giving him the actual facts and preparing to lead up to the events that took place.

"What exactly did happen?" Hans inquired attentively leaning forward in Renato's direction.

"They were trying to get in touch with some Mexican moon goddess. I think it was Ix Chel," Renato said with evident distaste.

"Yes, I am familiar with Ix Chel, the Mayan moon goddess. Beautiful and sad legend about her and Kinich Ahau, the sun god. The Mexicans are very fond of her."

"A while back, Sister Shiela, the coordinator, channeled her into one of the sisters, Lotta Biermann. It seems they had been doing that frequently. This time, however, something went awry, because a male entity that said his name was Abraxas suddenly took over. It was really demonic!" Renato exclaimed shaking his head as he squinted at Hans in distaste.

"Demonic! Surely you don't believe in demons, Renato." The archbishop laughed heartily. "We are no longer in the Dark Ages. This is the twenty-first century. Demons do not exist." Hans folded his hands smugly on his vest and looked at Renato in amusement.

Utterly abashed, Renato remained silent, hoping to change the topic of conversation. He cut off another bite of lamb and forced himself to eat it.

"So? What happened? I insist you tell me."

"It all got out of control. Sister Lotta started striking the coordinator in the face and was thrashing around rather violently. All the sisters and the laywomen present were terrified and were begging Sister Shiela to do something. She tried to bring Lotta out of it, but could not. Teresa Valdés, the president of the pastoral council, was there, and she took over and phoned Marco Lamadrid, and got him to come there at once and..."

"Wait," the archbishop interrupted holding up his right hand. "Who is Marco Lamadrid?" he asked with a quizzical look on his face and in his Prussian blue eyes.

"He is the priest who built Santiago."

"I am not familiar with any priest by that name in the archdiocese."

"Sexual allegations were made against him a few years back."

"*Ach so*! Were they proven to be true?"

"No, we paid off the people who made the allegations to silence them, so we would not have to go to court. Some of the accusers never even swore out depositions," Renato said with embarrassment. Then to exculpate himself, he said softly, "That was when Jan Zagan was vicar general. I really had very little to do with it. All the criminals in the country knew that bishops were giving large settlements to anyone who made an allegation of sexual abuse. They came forth in droves." Renato laid his knife and fork down on the table, unable to eat any more.

"Was there a canonical trial?"

"No. Marco Lamadrid kept insisting that he was innocent. Obviously because he did not trust us, he flew to Rome and hired a Roman Rota lawyer to represent him and managed to get his case transferred to Rome, putting it completely out of our jurisdiction. According to canon law, he had a right to have his case heard in Rome, so he appealed to the CDF—the former Holy Office of the Inquisition."

"And?" The archbishop was finishing up every scrap of lamb that was served him and all the vegetables as well.

"If they had tried his case, they would have found him innocent. His accusers had absolutely no evidence to substantiate their ridiculous accounts that were full of holes and lies." Renato was finding the conversation extremely tedious. He could feel his face getting hot, as he squirmed under the archbishop's interrogation.

"So?"

"Archbishop L'Abbadon phoned some of his friends in Rome and got the case sent back to us for trial. Zagan arranged for Monsignor Paul F. X. Linde to be the promoter of justice who would try the case. We knew that Linde had been a very outspoken enemy of Lamadrid for years. With him trying the case, we were sure he would find in our favor. You see we were determined to unfrock Lamadrid. We had to unfrock him. After we had paid all that money to silence his accusers, there was no way we could have him found innocent. We would have looked ridiculous. The *Rosanada News* would have crucified us. And if they had known we had given their money to a bunch of criminals, we would have lost the financial support of the people in the pews." Drops of perspiration were forming on his brow. He sighed deeply and continued with a whine in his voice. "We really had no choice, Hans. Surely you see that."

"You held a canonical trial here in Rosanada?" Hans asked with perplexity showing in his unflinching eyes.

"No, we were so thankful we did not have to. We escaped that. Lamadrid retired. You might say we forced him into retirement at sixty years of age. He knew he had no other choice. We had the deck stacked against him, and we held all the cards. We stripped him of everything. He lost his television ministries that were valued at a million dollars." Despising Marco Lamadrid's charismatic approach to the faith, Renato did not want to let Hans know how happy he personally had been to get him out of the priesthood.

Thoughtfully Hans Fuchs shook his head and smoothed his blonde graying hair at the temples. Then more to himself than to Renato he said, "*Traurig*. Really sad what the Church has come to." He thought a few moments and then added, "Now that you mention it, I remember seeing this Lamadrid on television. He preaches a damn good sermon. He is a charismatic—definitely not my approach—but nevertheless he is a good man. He deserved better treatment from the Church." Squinting from behind his large frame glasses, he asked: "You say the president of the pastoral council at Santiago phoned this Marco Lamadrid and asked for his help?"

"Yes, he is now the pastor of Grace Pentecostal Chapel here in Rosanada."

"The archdiocese lost a good man when they got rid of him. What happened when he came in response to their plea for help?"

"By commanding the entity to be gone in the name of Jesus Christ, he restored Lotta Biemann to her usual self. He also cautioned the sisters that if they did not all renounce their pagan practices, the one who called himself Abraxas would return."

Chuckling softly, the archbishop commented, "Another one who believes in demons. They simply do not exist," he said emphatically and smugly. "Lamadrid probably caused more fear in the convent by his exorcism and his insistence that the demonic influence would return. That was a very poor pastoral approach. When we go to the confirmation out there—I believe it is scheduled for next week—I personally will try to say a few words to the sisters to see if we can help them to heal so that they can get on with the beautiful ministry they exercise in the archdiocese. I am sure they have been under a terrible strain with the deaths of two of the nuns and Father Julian Parnell." The archbishop toyed with the chain of his pectoral cross that draped across his vest. Folding his hands in an attitude of prayer, he said, "I am grieved to lose that fine young priest. He was a priest after my own heart." Sadness crept over the archbishop as he spoke and was reflected in his facial demeanor.

Renato suddenly realized that he had more in common with the charismatic Marco Lamadrid than he did with the ultra liberal Hans Fuchs. Attempting to change the conversion, he said:

"It was certainly fortunate for us that the judge let Shannon out on bail. We have no one to send to Santiago as administrator to fill in for him."

"Yes I know. I was able to pull a few strings and got the judge to set bail for him. I did not suspend him and put him on administrative leave, because, I really can't imagine that he killed anyone."

The musicians and the belly dancers returned just as Ali and Abdul were bringing their dessert, which Hans assured him was one of his favorites—*shabiet*—layers of filo pastry shaped into a triangle and filled with custard. When the dance was finished, a swarthy woman wearing a luxurious blue silk flowing, diaphanous robe came into the salon privé with a box of Turkish cigars. Eagerly Hans took one of them, cut off the end and began puffing on it, as the woman lit it with a large bronze lighter. "Take a cigar, Renato. They are the best you can get," Hans insisted.

Trying to appear as a contented guest, Renato took a cigar although he detested them, cut off the end, as he has seen Hans do, and waited for the girl to light it. Drawing the acrid smoke into his mouth was very unpleasant for him, but he pretended to enjoy it, until he suddenly began coughing uncontrollably.

"What's the trouble, Renato? Not used to smoking cigars? Well you will get used to them. They are very enjoyable once you do. Go ahead and try it again." Hans urged him.

Again he puffed on the cigar, but he had to put it down. It was making him sick and a bit dizzy." He couldn't wait to get out of Al Amir and go home. It was already half past four, but Hans was not about to leave until he had finished his cigar. Then he called Fritz to bring the limo.

With a flourish he signed the tab for the meal, including large tips for the maitre d, the waiters, the belly dancers and the musicians, and had it sent to the archdiocese.

When Fritz finally delivered him at Casa St. Popola it was already after five, and John Bugumil was stretched out on the sofa listening to Debussy's *Prélude à l'après-midi d'un faune* from his collection of CDs. His relationship with Bugumil was one of the best things that ever happened to him. A willing listener and always ready to support him, John was a true companion who understood him well. Although Bugumil did not like the liberal theology of the archbishop, and hoped with Renato to see the Church return to the way it was before the Second Vatican Council, he was like a chameleon in that he could always adapt to his environment. Perhaps his adaptablility was due to his bi-ritual and bi-cultural orientation. Coming from a Slovak family, he belonged originally to the Byzantine Catholic Church.

When Renato began telling Bugumil about his visit to Al Amir, he turned down the volume on the CD player so they could talk. "I don't like Fuchs' theology either. He is a strong advocate of Bultmann's demythologizing of the Holy Scripture. I heard him give a talk once in which he said that he did not believe that the miracles in the Bible really happened, that there were no Magi and no slaughter of the Holy Innocents, and that Jesus had no consciousness of who he was until late in his ministry." His hazel eyes were clouded with doubt and disbelief.

"I know. I have known for some time that he even advocates using the term "transignification" instead of "transubstantiation," Renato replied as he began undressing. "What gets me the most is that he does not seem to care that the sisters at Santiago were trying to channel a Mexican moon goddess. With his interest and university degree in Comparative Religion, the introduction of what we would call pagan practices into Catholicism doesn't seem to bother him at all. I don't like it at all, John. "Renato poured a jigger of bourbon into a glass. Having been in United States for quite some years, he now drank like an American.

"Well, at least he understands about our relationship and doesn't trouble us about it. So let's just live in peace, grateful for the happiness we have," John said smiling at him with a twinkle in his gentle, hazel eyes.

"I just wish I did not have to go to the confirmation out at Santiago next week. It gives me feelings of anxiety just to think about it, but Hans insists that I go with him. After all, three people, one of them a priest, have been murdered there."

"I think you are unduly concerned. You have nothing to worry about," John said trying to console him.

"I don't think Shannon is guilty. In my opinion, the killer is still loose. I think there is plenty to worry about. I am going to ask for police surveillance of the ceremony. I'll go. I have to, but I will have my Barreta in the pocket of my jacket.

26

Mel

Monsignor was watching the evening news on television, as Mel strolled into the living room of the rectory. He was fortunate to have Petit helping him at Santiago. Rock solid and a bit of a workhorse, Petit could be relied on, otherwise they would not have been able to manage without Father Julian. One of the deacons that the chancery sent them was good at counseling and was able to pick up some of Julian's work with the people who needed that kind of help. How anyone could think that he had killed Father Parnell was beyond his comprehension. Yet, he had been charged with the murder and was extremely fortunate to be out on bail. Nevertheless, he was having trouble sleeping. Sometimes it took him over two hours to fall asleep, after he went to bed. So tonight he decided to go jogging around the premises of Santiago, hoping that the exercise and cold arctic air would help him to sleep. With Valin Vogel patrolling the grounds, he felt safe behind the tall iron fence that Marco Lamadrid had built to encircle the grounds and keep out the criminal element that roamed in the surrounding neighborhood, which had a reputation for being one of the worst in the archdiocese. A real watchdog, Valin Vogel kept close surveillance over the premises.

"I am going out jogging," he announced to Monsignor Petit as he fetched his winter boots, black leather gloves, gray wool scarf, and heavy down jacket from the coat closet by the entrance door and began putting them on.

"*Eh bien.* You better wrap up good," Petit said during a commercial break in his television news program. "I was over to the parish hall awhile ago. It is bitter cold and there is strong wind blowing with more snow on the way." He puffed contentedly on his meerschaum pipe as clouds of smoke billowed up from his rich aromatic tobacco filling the room.

"I won't be gone long. If anyone calls, I'll be back soon," Mel replied as he walked out the door into the night.

The sting of the wind on his face was bracing. Without a moon or any stars visible in the sky, the night was very dark. Snow was beginning to fall with the weather man calling for a further accumulation of about six inches overnight. The walk in front of the rectory was clear. He had seen Vogel plowing it earlier in the evening. Since there were patches of ice on the walkway leading in the direction of the parish hall and the school, he decided that jogging was not a good idea, so he began walking briskly under the tall overarching oaks.

A sudden noise in a branch directly above his head startled him. Shining his flashlight upward, he spotted a large owl that began hooting as its privacy was invaded, and then flapping his wings flew wildly away. As he continued walking in the direction of the parish hall, he passed the convent. Christmas lights twinkled from the living room window, but no one was to be seen. Except for a stray black dog that went running ahead of him in the direction of the school, the grounds of Santiago were completely deserted.

Suddenly his flashlight beam picked up something strange on the sidewalk on the drifting snow. He stopped walking and bending over looked more closely. There was no doubt about it. There was fresh blood staining the sidewalk, and the fresh snow that had blown onto it was tinged in red. Shining his flashlight around the area, he noticed that there was a dark hump lying in the snow and partially buried by it. With the snow almost to the tops of his boots, he plowed through it to get a closer look at the object that was lying about ten feet from the sidewalk. As he drew nearer to the dark mass that lay at his feet, he could see that it was the body of a man. Turning the spot of light on the man's face, he saw that it was Valin Vogel lying there utterly still in the drifting snow. Judging from the amount of snow that had accumulated on him, he had been there for some time.

Whipping his cell phone from the pocket of his down jacket, he phoned the police.

"I think there has been another murder committed here at Santiago Church. I just came across the body of our security guard lying in the snow in front of the parish hall. He looks dead."

Within minutes Detectives Zadek and Rogers were on the scene. After Vogel's body was removed and the crime scene roped off, they read him his rights, told him to put his hands behind his back, snapped the handcuffs on him, and pushed him into the back of their Toyota patrol car.

When they got to police headquarters, they allowed him to phone his lawyer and Monsignor Petit. Forte promised to come to see him the first thing the next morning.

When the jailer closed the steel bars of his cell with a loud metallic clang, he commented: "This time, Shannon, you will not get out here.

They let you our before and look what happened.—another man found dead at your place. Three people killed at Santiago and you found them all three. Mighty suspicious, I'd say."

After a sleepless night and a light breakfast, Mel looked forward to seeing his attorney. Shortly after nine, a jailer came and told him that someone was waiting to see him and led him into a room that had only a table and two chairs. As soon as he had sat down at the table, the door to the room opened and his visitor entered.

Expecting to see Cristian Forte, he was very much surprised to see Archbishop Hans Fuchs. Rising to his feet, he took the archbishop's hand in his and was getting ready to kiss his episcopal ring, when the archbishop stopped him.

"That's not necessary, Father Mel. I came to see if there is anything I could do to help you."

Amazed that the archbishop took time to visit him in jail, he said, "Thank you, Archbishop, for your concern." Mel knew that Archbishop L'Abbadon, his predecessor, would never have made the effort to visit anyone in jail.

"Just call me Hans. I am your brother, I believe in

you, Mel. I know you did not kill anyone. I am sure you will be vindicated." Raising his hand in blessing, he departed as swiftly as he had arrived.

Waiting for the jailer to come and return him to his cell, Mel was surprised again when Cristian Forte entered, as soon as the archbishop was gone and took the chair across the table from him.

"Sorry, Father Mel but there is absolutely no hope of getting you out on bail this time," he said laying his briefcase on the table. "I got the details on the death of Valin Vogel from the Sergeant on duty. It seems he was shot in his left temple with a nine millimeter bullet that went out the other side of his head, just behind his right ear, causing instant death. There was a small amount of bleeding—perhaps you saw it on the snow. They estimate that he had been dead about two hours when you found him. The police have been trying to find the murder weapon, thinking that perhaps the murderer would want to get rid of it, so it could not be found in his possession. They checked the garbage dumpster going through all the garbage from the rectory, school, convent, and parish hall, but found nothing."

"You have Gian Perdini keeping tabs on what goes on at Santiago? Did he see anything unusual last night about the time Vogel was killed?" Mel asked anxiously as he pushed his black wavy hair back off his forehead.

"Not really. There was a meeting in the parish hall during the evening. Some of the sisters were there and a few laywomen. Whoever shot Vogel must have used a silencer, since no one reports hearing a gunshot. Perdini stopped in the convent and talked to the sisters and in the rectory and questioned Monsignor Petit, but none of them had heard or seen anything unusual."

Mel put his head in his hands with his elbows on the table and sighed deeply.

"Don't look so discouraged, Father Mel. I do have some news to report."

Mel looked at him expectantly, but not really hoping for any news that would lift his spirits. "What is it, Cristian?"

"Megan McGrath was about eight weeks pregnant and they discovered that Father Julian was responsible for it. After they got that information from the McGrath woman's computer, they arrested Parnell for her murder. Circumstantial evidence, you understand."

"So now Julian is dead and I am their only suspect," Mel said slowly with discouragement and dejection sounding in his voice.

"That's not all they have discovered. They also impounded Parnell's computer and found a message on it from Diane Deladier who died recently from hemorrhaging after an abortion." Forte grimaced as he spoke these words. "Deplorable," he added.

"Yes, I had heard that was the cause of her tragic death." Mel replied. "Why was she writing to Julian? Did she want psychological counseling from him?"

"No, she wrote to tell him—it was about a week before she died—that she was breaking their relationship off and that she would not see him anymore. The police have no proof, but they suspect Julian was the one who got her pregnant also. Since she admitted to having a relationship with him, the police have reason to believe that Parnell got her pregnant also, although they have no proof. Just more circumstantial evidence, but they have very little else to go on."

After reflecting a few moments on this bit of news, Mel said, "Father Julian was gone many evenings. He said he spent them in his family home. I had no idea that he was involved with women."

"He wouldn't be the first priest to have trouble with Punch and Judy," Cristian said as he looked at Julian sympathetically. "We will keep working on your case. Perhaps the Vogel murder will give us some more clues to help us find the killer and get you back to the parish, Father Mel."

Shortly after Forte had gone and Mel had been returned to his cell, the jailer announced that he had still another visitor who insisted on speaking with him—a Monsignor Petit, the jailer said. Once more he was led into a room simply furnished with a table and two chairs where he could talk to his visitor who was already waiting for him to appear.

"*Bonjour*, Father Mel," Monsignor greeted him extending his hand and clasping his warmly. "I just came to tell you not to worry about anything. I am taking care of everything at Santiago. Everything is under control," he said, paused and then added, "as well as can be expected under the circumstances."

Closely observing the monsignor, Mel noticed that he looked older and his frail body was showing the signs of aging. Recent events were taking their toll on him. Thank you, Monsignor, I am sure you are doing a great job."

"Since the news of the death of Valin Vogel was front

page on today's *Sunday Rosanada News*," Petit continued "Mass attendance was way off this morning. People are afraid and I'm sure that many will not come to church until the murderer of the three victims is apprehended. The deacons that the VG sent us are helping out as much as they can, but of course they cannot celebrate the sacraments. I came here today to see if there is anything you need. Is there anything I can bring you from the rectory?"

"Yes, I'd like to have my breviary and my Mass kit. I want to say Mass here in my jail cell. Bring me some wine—get a bottle out of the closet in the office in the rectory. And bring me some hosts."

"*Tiens! Tiens!* I figured you would want those things, Father, so I already brought them with me today. I left them with the sergeant at the front desk out there. The officer said they would check them out and then bring them to you. If there is anything else you want, just let me know, and I will take care of it."

About an hour after Monsignor Petit had left, the jailer brought him his breviary, Mass kit, and the wine and the hosts. Kneeling on the cold stone floor beside the cot in his cell, Father Mel turned to God in prayer, seeking Him more ardently than he ever had before in his entire life. Saying the prayers of the Mass he consecrated the bread and wine that Monsignor Petit had brought him on the little table provided In his cell, He was no longer alone. Christ was with him stilling his fears, comforting him in his darkness, and easing his pain.

27
Monsignor Petit

With the pastor in jail accused of murdering his vicar, Santiago, under the circumstances, was as ready for the confirmation ceremony as it could be. Since it was only nine days before Christmas, the traditional evergreen advent wreath with the three purple candles and one rose one sat on a large stand to the right of the ambo. Midnight blue banners depicting the stars that twinkled over Bethlehem to light the way for the Magi as they sought the newborn King of the Jews hung on the walls above the altar. As Christmas drew nearer the stars were changed, each week becoming a bit larger.

Not only were many young adults to be confirmed, there were also a large number of men and women who were to be admitted to the sacraments, so that they would be able to celebrate Christmas in the embrace of the Church.

When he discussed the music for the ceremony with Sister Shiela, she told him that she herself had selected it. Assuring him that Sister Lotta was a very talented musician, she informed him that she was having her harp moved from the convent chapel to the sanctuary of Santiago church for the occasion, and that Sister Lotta would play several solo pieces on the instrument for the ceremony.

Snow was falling all day as they got ready for the confirmation that was to be held at night so that as many people as possible would be free to attend. Although it was still the liturgical season of advent, greens were hung around the church. The hanging of the greens was always greeted at Santiago with joy and many people came out to put the holly and fir boughs around the church. The actual Christmas decorations would not be put up until Christmas Eve, when the empty Christmas crèche would be placed in the sanctuary waiting for the Christ Child to be born.

When Monsignor Petit came into the church late in the afternoon on the day of the confirmation to make sure that everything was in readiness, the fragrance of the firs filled the sanctuary with the pungent scent of Christmas. To the right of the altar stood a special high back chair for the archbishop and a somewhat smaller, but similar chair, to the left of the altar for Bishop Del'Ano.

With Nirvana's help, he had arranged a small dinner party to be held for the archbishop and Bishop Del'Ano at 6:00 in the evening before the confirmation at 8:00. Because the archbishop was a good friend of the provincial of the Adorines and had brought the sisters to the archdiocese, as a courtesy to them, he invited Sister Shiela, since she was the coordinator and Sister Lotta Biermann, since she was of German parentage and was going to play the harp at the ceremony.

Upon their arrival at precisely at 5:30, the time designated for cocktails, Nirvana ushered Archbishop

Fuchs and Bishop Del'Ano into the living room of the rectory where poinsettias on the cocktail table hinted at the coming Feast of the Nativity, despite the sadness and gloom that pervaded Santiago. Since it was the Christmas season, Nirvana had filled the crystal punchbowl with eggnog and put it on the cocktail table that stood before the sofa in the living room. Just as Monsignor Petit was pouring a cup of it for Archbishop Fuchs, Sister Shiela arrived wearing a bright red suit with a ruffled blouse trimmed in green. Following at her heals was Sister Lotta Biermann, dressed more sedately in a dark green suit.

"Good evening, Archbishop," Sister Shiela greeted, as she entered the living room. When she saw Renato Del'Ano, she greeted him with the nod of her head. Looking as if she had just come from the beauty salon, her hair, no longer hennaed, but now the color of ebony, was coiffed in an intricate fashion piled up high on her head.

After pouring herself a cup of eggnog, Sister Shiela took a seat on the sofa beside Monsignor Petit and began asking him about his experiences in Morocco. When he made only brief responses to her questions, she turned to Archbishop Fuchs and began discussing the Church in Europe with him as she sipped her eggnog. Sister Lotta sat quietly by the fireplace.

"I was in Europe last summer," Shiela said, "where I attended a conference in Cologne and had the opportunity to travel extensively in France, Germany and Italy," She smiled at Archbishop Fuchs her most charming smile. "I couldn't help but notice that the churches were mostly deserted and the people who were in them were old. At the conference they talked about how we are in the post-modern age. Some even described it as the post-Christian age."

Monsignor Petit saw that Bishop Del'Ano was bristling as Sheila said this. Then looking over his punch cup from which he was sipping eggnog, he stated emphatically: "When I was in Europe on His Excellency's last *ad limina* visit, I saw lots of people praying in the Italian churches, I think you are mistaken with the term "post-Christian, Sister."

"On the contrary," Shiela protested arching her eyebrows, "there is evidence that many Europeans have embraced simple religions that get them back to nature. Many have been influenced by the New Age movement and are seeking to find the divine within themselves, because they have become totally disillusioned with organized religion."

Warming to the conversation about a topic that was obviously close to his heart, the archbishop remarked: "That is quite true. In my study of comparative religions, I find that basically we are all searching for the same things. There is a lot of truth to be found in all religions. One of our great German writers Gotthold Ephraim Lessing wrote a play called *Nathan der Weise*, published way back in 1779. Perhaps you are familiar with it, Sister Lotta, since you know German. In English it is called *Nathan the Wise*. I like the parable of the ring in this play. Let me tell you about it. In the play Nathan relates a parable to the Muslim Saladin when he asked him which is the true religion. In the parable an heirloom ring that has the wondrous ability to make its owner pleasing in the sight of God has been handed down from father to son for generations. Finally a father has to choose which of his three sons that he loved equally would get the ring. Not knowing what to do, he promised the ring to each of them.

"So what did he do?" Renato asked as he set his empty cup on the cocktail table, walked to the fireplace, and warmed his hands, chaffing them briskly.

"Well," said the archbishop, as all eyes were on him waiting for him to explain, "wishing to keep his promise to each of them and to find a solution to his dilemma, the father had two replicas made of the original ring, and as he lay dying, gave one of the rings to each son. When the brothers quarreled about who got the real ring, a very wise judge told them that each of them was to live in such a way that the powers of the ring they possessed were to be proven true." The archbishop cleared his throat and smoothed his graying blonde hair at the temples. There was a twinkle in his eyes as he looked from one to another of his dinner partners to see how they reacted to his story.

"So," asked Renato. "I don't get the point of the story."

"*Ach so*! It is very simple. Nathan who is relating the story to the Saladin compares the ring to religion, saying that by analogy each of us must live by the religion we have received. And, of course, we must be tolerant of the beliefs of others," the archbishop concluded as he finished his cup of eggnog and set the empty cup on the cocktail table beside Renato's.

Finding the conversation very much against his

traditional Catholic views, Renato remarked, "I still hold the old view of outside the Church there is no salvation. Bonifatius VIII promulgated it as dogma and at least ten popes have reaffirmed it, including Leo XII and Pius XII."

Monsignor Petit could see that Bishop Del'Ano was deeply annoyed by the turn of the conversation and was bristling with suppressed anger.

"Come now, Renato," Archbishop Fuchs, cajoled, "This is the twenty-first century, not the nineteenth when people believed such things. There is going to be a convergence of all world religions in the glorious new order that will come about, if not in our life time, shortly thereafter." He crossed his legs and leaned back in the sofa.

"Oh, I couldn't agree more completely" Sister Shiela responded as her green eyes studied the face of the archbishop. "And Teilhard de Chardin teaches that humankind will be gloriously transformed in this new age."

Folding his hands together and resting his chin on his upstretched fingers, the archbishop declared: "We have made a lot of progress towards convergence. Why Tenzin Gyatso, the fourteenth Dalai Lama, the spiritual leader of Tibetian Budhism visited Pope John Paul eight times. That is more than any other dignitary ever visited him. It is inevitable. After all, we are all God's children."

Monsignor Petit could see that Bishop Del'Ano was silently fuming, as he listened to the archbishop's comments. "Only if Christ is our brother, can we claim God as Father," Del'Ano stated dogmatically.

Observing the way that Bishop Del'Ano was responding to the archbishop's remarks, Sister Shiela exclaimed with evident enthusiasm: "Yes, I agree with you, Hans. At the meeting for a world day of prayer that John Paul II held in Assisi in 1986 there were 120 representatives from different religions and Christian denominations present. There was even a Voodoo priest."

Noticing that Bishop Del'Ano had very little to say, the archbishop got up and walked over to the fireplace where Del'Ano was still standing with his back to the fire.

"You haven't said very much, Renato, go ahead and tell us your opinion. I never try to squelch you. You are free to express yourself without fear of any reprisals from me," the archbishop spoke with great sincerity.

"To speak the truth, "Del'Ano replied, "I applauded Cardinal Biffi who refused to take part in the interfaith prayers for world peace at Assisi. I don't see how we can join in prayer with pagans and infidels such as the Muslims."

When Nirvana rang the dinner bell summoning the guests to table, Monsignor Petit lead the way, glad that the bell had put an end to the conversation. After the archbishop, sitting at the head of the long mahogany table, said the blessing, the conversation picked up instantly where it had left off with Shiela commenting:

"Cardinal Biffi is a bigot. He is the one who claims that the Antichrist is among us and that he is a fascinating personality who is charming, a vegetarian, a pacifist, an environmentalist, and an advocate of animals' rights. I say bosh!" Shiela nibbled on one of the large pink shrimp in her appetizer. "It was a good day for the Church, when he retired as Archbishop of Bologna!"

At the mention of Cardinal Biffi, Renato stopped eating and said somewhat vehemently: "As I understand it, Cardinal Biffi said that the Antichrist would be a man who promotes vague and fashionable spiritual values, rather than solid doctrine, that he would espouse a feel-good type of religion concerned with causes such as ecology and humanitarian aid, deceiving people into believing that such is the true faith." Then turning to Sister Lotta who was seated on his left, Bishop Del'Ano asked, "What do you think, Sister Lotta?"

The young nun who had been very quiet since they arrived for dinner, smiled sweetly at the bishop, and said, "My opinions don't really matter, but I think ecology and humanitarian aid are both very important. We have had many conferences on preserving the environmental resources of Mother Earth, Isn't that right, Sister," she asked putting the conversation ball in Shiela's court.

Realizing that he should have considered more carefully before inviting the liberated nuns to dinner with the very conservative Bishop Del'Ano and the liberal Hans Fuchs, Monsignor Petit tried to steer the conversation into more agreeable topics. They were definitely not congenial dinner partners. In fact, Sister Shiela and Bishop Del'Ano were sullenly glaring at each other across the table. The bishop had barely touched his crab imperial.

When the dinner was over, Monsignor Petit who was in the kitchen was able to overhear Bishop Del'Ano as he lingered at the table as did Shiela while the others went back into the living doom and were listening to the evening news on television, and were consequently unable to hear the conversation taking place in the dining room.

"Sister Shiela," Del'Ano said forcefully as he tried to stare her down across the dinner table, "I am appalled by your beliefs and practices and I intend to use the full force of my office as Vicar General of the Rosanada Archdiocese to get you out here and bring in some nuns that dress like nuns and act like consecrated women instead a bunch of harpies and tarts. It is simply deplorable that the McGrath woman who was murdered was pregnant and the other nun that died bled to death as the result of an abortion! I tell you to your face that I intend to speak to Excellency Bishop Roberto Cosimo Martino, the papal nuncio, recommending that the Ardorines be dealt with severely. I also am drafting a letter to the Cardinal Prefect of the Congregation for Institutes of Consecrated Life in Rome, informing him and the Curia of the dissolute life of the Ardorines. I shall have it ready to send it to him within the week." Del'Ano was toying with his dinner knife as he spoke.

With fire blazing in her dark catlike green eyes, Shiela lashed out at him, "People like you are destroying the Church." Her voice was getting sharp and bitter, as she surveyed his feminine features and slender hands. "You obviously don't like women." Hissing boldly, she leaned across the table in his face and said bitterly: "I don't give a damn what you do. I am fed up with your phallocratic establishment. I've had enough!" Pushing her chair back violently and rising to her feet, she left him sitting at the table and went to join the archbishop and Lotta in the living room.

Before the situation could become any more inflammatory, Monsignor Petit decided it was time for his intervention.

'I think it is time for you, Sisters, to go to the church and get the harp tuned up."

"Gladly," Shiela agreed, obviously anxious to get away from the company of Bishop Del'Ano.

"Since it is still snowing and it is accumulating rapidly, take the underground tunnel to the church," Monsignor directed as he escorted the women to the kitchen and opened the door into the subterranean passageways. "Here take this flashlight, you will need it." When the two women were gone, Monsignor Petit joined the men in the living room where they continued watching the evening news.

When the time came for them all to go the church for the confirmation, Monsignor Petit escorted the group to the kitchen, opened the door in the pantry leading to the tunnel. Providing them each with a flash light, he led the way down the dimly lit stairs and through the dark passageway.

Despite the continued snowfall, the church was filled with people that had come to witness Archbishop Fuchs and Bishop Del'Ano administer the sacrament of confirmation. As they processed down the center aisle to the sanctuary, the choir was singing an invocation to the Holy Spirit. Monsignor Petit had to admit that Archbishop Fuchs cut a handsome figure in his gold chasuble and miter. As soon as the clergy had taken their places in the sanctuary, the music director led the congregation in singing the litany of the saints, as one by one, they called on the holy men and women of God to pray for them.

From when he was seated in the sanctuary, Monsignor Petit could observe Sister Lotta Biermann as she took her place on what used to be called the epistle side of the church directly across from the ambo.

Dressed in a frothy two piece, blue gown of gossamer silk, she looked angelic with her blond hair and her smiling blue eyes, as she began plucking the strings on the great harp, caressing them gently. Encouraging her to play her best, Sister Shiela was sitting in the front row right in front of her.

Immediately in front of the ambo and appearing to be enjoying the music immensely were all the confirmandi with the children seated in the very front rows and the adults behind them. Since the harp was always one of his favorite musical instruments, Monsignor Petit was listening intently as Sister Lotta plucked the strings, playing Mozart's *Ave Verum Corpus*, although he would have preferred the music of a French composer. He noticed that Hans Fuchs seemed to be enjoying Mozart immensely.

Suddenly for no apparent reason, Sister Lotta stopped playing, pushed the harp back away from her, rose to her feet and yelled at the top of her lungs: "Hans fucks! Hans fucks!" Leaving the harp and dancing around the sanctuary, she came to stand right in front of the archbishop, "Hans fucks!" she yelled while pointing at him and cackling like an old crone.

Startled the archbishop leaned over in his chair and whispered to Monsignor Petit: "*Verückt!* The woman is crazy. Absolutely nuts. Get her out of here—at once!"

Monsignor Petit rose to his feet and signaled for the ushers to come and remove Lotta from the sanctuary. As the ushers came closer, Archbishop Fuchs, fuming with anger called to them:

"Get her out of here and take her to the sacristy NOW!"

When the ushers approached Lotta who was now dancing all around the sanctuary, they tried to grab her, but she alluded them as she kept shouting as loud as she could: "Hans fucks! Hans fucks!" Then kicking off her shoes, she yelled in a strong masculine voice, "I am Abraxas!" Pulling the top of her organza dress off over her head, and completely naked from the waist up, except for a very seductive black lace brassiere, she began mocking the archbishop by yelling in German: "*Hans fickt! Hans fickt! Der alte Fuchs fickt!*" Then quickly unhooking her brassière, she took it hand and swung it around in the air high over her head, with her firm young breasts shining at the archbishop like a couple of headlights.

Immediately the ushers converged on her, ready to carry her out, but as they approached, she threw herself down on the floor, stretched out, and defiantly yelled at them.

"I won't go, I won't go," she screamed. "You can't make me!" Then as loud as she could, she yelled: "The old fox fucks! *Er ist ein Scheisshund!*"

"Lotta," Sister Shiela jumped to her feet and called

out to her with all the authority she could muster as coordinator of the Ardorines: "Lotta, come here at once!"

Undaunted by Sister Shiela's command, Lotta called out to the children who were to be confirmed: "Come dance with me, kids! Come up here! We'll have a real blast!"

"No! Stay where you are," Shiela commanded the children, as some of them began to respond to Lotta's invitation. "Stay back!" A number of parents came and grabbing their children by the hands, rushed for the exits. Again Shiela called out to Lotta to come to her.

Ignoring Shiela completely, Sister Lotta began kicking the men that tried to pick her up. When four of them finally succeeded in getting her off the floor, she began cursing them, and screaming. To the man who was holding her left arm, she yelled: "Pablo, your wife is a whore—*eine Hure*. When he cringed at these words, she laughed at him. To the man on her right: "Henry, does your wife know about the blonde waitress you fuck every Tuesday night?" As the men showed their embarrassment because of her accusations, she began laughing hideously and mocking them mercilessly. "Ha!" she exclaimed to the other two men who were holding her: "'I know your sins too, Ron! And yours, Joe. You too cheat on your wives! You will go to hell for your sins! You are damned forever, and you will be with me in hell for all eternity."

As they struggled to cover Lotta's naked breasts with one of their jackets, she squirmed, making it impossible for them to put her arms into the jacket's sleeves. When they succeeded in wrapping it around her shoulders, she screamed, "*Achtung! Achtung! Ich muss pissen!* Not understanding a work of German, the ushers were totally dumfounded, when she deluged them profusely, soaking them and the red sanctuary carpet with foul smelling urine.

As the ushers struggled to carry her out of the sanctuary to the sacristy, she twisted and turned, writhing in their grasp, trying to free herself. Suddenly she stopped trying to get free and vomited violently, regurgitating her dinner all over them and the sanctuary floor. "I am Abraxas," she yelled in a deep masculine voice. "I will see you in hell!"

As the people rose to their feet and watched horrified with many rushing for the exits, the men dragged Sister Lotta, who was spread out on the floor with blood gushing from her nose, from the church into the sacristy with pandemonium breaking loose in the church.

After one of the men got a mop and cleaned up the mess in the sanctuary, Monsignor Petit signaled to the choir to begin singing and bring order back into the congregation.

Taking control of the situation and going to the ambo, Archbishop Fuchs began to address the congregation with all the force of his office: "Quiet, please." Motioning with both hands for them to get silent, he said: "The woman is very sick. We have called for an ambulance and she will be well taken care of. I apologize for this interruption of our confirmation that really hasn't even yet begun. We will continue now as if nothing untoward has happened."

Monsignor Petit noticed that Sister Shiela had rushed

into the sacristy to help with Sister Lotta. When the confirmation was over, he went into the sacristy and both Sisters were gone. No doubt, he figured, Sister Shiela had gone in the ambulance with Sister Lotta to the hospital. Later he learned that Sister Lotta had been taken to the psychiatric ward of Divine Providence Hospital where they administered a maximum dose of midazolam by injection in order to achieve complete sedation.

Escorting Archbishop Fuchs and Bishop Del'Ano through the subterranean tunnels back to the rectory, Monsignor Petit apologized profusely for Sister Lotta's behavior.

"It was not your fault, Pierre," Fuchs said. "The woman is obviously mentally disturbed."

"I think she is possessed." Renato insisted as he went to the coat closet. Monsignor Petit noticed that he slipped something into the pocket of his top coat as he began putting it on. "Pius XII said Hitler and Stalin were both possessed and he tried and failed to exorcise them both from a distance—which is almost impossible to do."

When he saw Bishop Del'Ano getting ready to leave, Monsignor Petit addressed the archbishop formally. He was determined that he would never call him Hans.

"Archbishop," he said, "the snow has accumulated far more than was anticipated and the weather man is calling for perhaps six inches more before morning. I suggest you stay the night. We have plenty of room here," Petit invited.

Glancing out the large casement window of the rectory at the street, Archbishop Fuchs said, "Thank you for your hospitality. We would be pleased to stay the night, but I just realized that I left my pectoral cross in the sacristy. When I was vesting I removed it from my jacket pocket and laid it on the cabinet there." The archbishop walked to the fireplace and stood with his back to the fire enjoying the warmth it generated. Bishop Del'Ano took off his overcoat and returned it to the closet.

"Let me run over and get your cross for you," Bishop Del'Ano volunteered, as he started walking out of the living room to go into the kitchen to the door in the panty that led down to the tunnels.

"It is quite safe there—*vraiement*," Monsignor Petit said, "We can get it in the morning. No one will bother it."

"I'd really like to have it," Hans Fuchs said glancing at Bishop Del'Ano. "It has special significance to me. My parents gave it to me when I was consecrated a bishop."

Always trying to curry the favor of the archbishop, Renato Del'Ano said, "Monsignor Petit, if you give me the key to the sacristy door that leads into the tunnels, I'll go get it. It is really no trouble."

Taking the keys, Renato entered the stairway in the pantry, and calling back over his shoulder said, "I'll be back in just a few minutes."

28

Bishop Del'Ano

Renato was glad to get away from the others for a little while. After the disgusting performance of Sister Lotta Biermann, hopping around the sanctuary and shouting obscenities at the top of her lungs, he now had more ammunition to fire over to the Congregation for Institutes of Consecrated Life in Rome. Once they heard of this performance, together with the abortion of Sister Diane Deladier and the pregnancy of Sister Megan McGrath, they would put an end to their strange feminist practices, and hopefully this would destroy the congregation of Ardorines that had been dwindling in numbers in recent years.

As he made his way through the tunnel, he thought he heard someone walking in another part of the subterranean system. When he stopped to listen to determine if there were someone else in the tunnels, the sound of footsteps likewise stopped. After waiting a couple seconds, he proceeded in the direction of the church. When he came to an intersection of the tunnels, he thought he glimpsed someone standing at some distance in the tunnel that led to the parish hall and convent. Because the tunnels were dimly lit, he could not be sure. As a wave of terror began to rise up in his being, he searched in his jacket pocket for his Barretta. It wasn't there! Suddenly he remembered that after they returned to the rectory from the confirmation, he had put it in his overcoat pocket, because it was heavy too carry around. Besides, he thought they were going to be leaving right away to return to the archiepiscopal residence where he would drop off the archbishop before returning to Casa St. Popola.

Walking faster, he reached the steps leading up to the sacristy climbing them two at a time. Using the key Monsignor Petit had designated, he quickly entered the sacristy, turning on the lights just inside the door. Immediately he spotted the archbishop's pectoral cross on the cabinet, picked it up and put it in his pocket and began the return trip to the rectory.

The tunnels seemed completely deserted now. With fear gnawing at his mind, he quickened his pace. Something moved up ahead of him at the point where the tunnel to the parish hall and convent branched off. He froze in his tracks for a minute. It was only a mouse. Heaving a sigh of relief, he continued and approached the place where he could look down the tunnel that led to the convent. There *was* someone there. A dark figure was coming toward him. It was a woman dressed totally in black. As she came closer, he saw that it was Sister Shiela. When she was about fifty feet from him, she called out, "Don't move or I will shoot!"

When she was about twenty-five feet away, he saw that she had a gun in her hand equipped with a silencer and she was pointing it at him.

"I have already killed three people. Now I will kill you

to shut you up. You won't be sending any reports to Rome or anywhere else." She took closer aim with the gun.

Sizing up the danger he was in, Renato decided to make a run for it. A moving target would be harder for her to hit than one that was standing motionless. As he ran as fast as he could toward the rectory, a bullet whizzed past his head. Pain ripped though his arm. Realizing that he had been struck, he tried to run faster. Then pain tore at his chest. He was shot in the back. Reaching the stairs that led up to the rectory pantry, he somehow managed to climb them holding onto the railing. Opening the door, he quite literally fell into the panty. "Help!" he cried, seared with excruciating pain.

Instantly Archbishop Fuchs and Monsignor Petit were at his side, bending over him.

"What happened, Renato?"

"Sister Shiela shot me. She is the killer! She is the killer! She just told me! She shot me. Call the police before she gets away." Renato heard Monsignor Petit make the call.

With great difficulty breathing, Renato saw his whole life pass though his mind. Memories of Torricella flooded his consciousness. As he felt his strength ebb, he wondered what would become of his aging mother, if he died. Only one other person would miss him and even care that he died—John Bugumil. It seemed so unfair. He was too young to die. He had always hoped to rise higher in the hierarchy. He thought of his sins. It had been a long time since he had gone to confession. "Hans," he whispered softly, "Hear my confession."

"Jawohl, "Hans said drawing closer to his vicar general. "I am here. Go ahead."

"So many sins—sins of the flesh—sins of the spirit." it was becoming difficult for him to speak. "It has been 5 years since my last confession. Since that time …" It was as if he were walking though a tunnel with darkness swirling around him. Speech failed him.

29

Zeek

"Come on, Rogers, let's go! There has been another shooting at Santiago. This time the victim lived long enough to identify the killer as Sister Shiela, the head nun out there. Monsignor Petit phoned to say that she was trying to get away in the convent van, but having difficulty starting the engine, because of the cold weather." Zeek zipped up his trench coat and headed for the car.

When they pulled up at the convent minutes later, Sister Shiela had the van running, and when she saw them, revved up the engine and took off down the street.

Following closely after her with the siren on the Toyota blaring, Zeek was determined to catch her. As she headed up the river, he decided that she was headed for the mountains. Snowplows had cleared the highway, and the crews with salt and cinders had done their work.

"We will outrun her easily," commented Rogers. "The van has absolutely no traction and we have chains on the Toyota."

Snow continued to fall as they left Rosanada and began the climb up the winding road to the summit of the mountain ridge. When she reached, the top Shiela turned onto a mountain road that followed the mountain tops northward into the national forest.

'Hold on to you hat, Rogers, this is going to be a rough ride," Zeek exclaimed as he kept in hot pursuit of the convent van.

Shiela continued to keep ahead of them, but they were gaining on her. As she rounded a sharp curve, the van began to spin out of control.

"The woman is crazy to drive that fast on these icy roads," Zeek remarked as he sped up the Toyota, hoping to catch up with her.

"If we get close enough, I can shoot out her tires," Rogers said as they skidded around the curve.

"If we did that, she would lose control of the van and crash. I don't want her dead. I want her to stand trial for her crimes. Justice demands that she pay for what she has done," Zeek replied as he kept the tail lights of the van in sight.

Faster and faster Shiela drove, narrowly escaping running off the road, as she turned a sharp curve. Suddenly another car was coming towards her, forcing her to slow down and stay on her side of the road, instead of driving down the middle. When she put on the brakes to slow the van, it began to skid. Zeek could see that she was fighting for control of the clumsy vehicle. Unable to get the traction she needed, she was unable to negotiate a curve and was heading over an embankment.

Holding his breath, Zeek watched as the van disappeared over the hill. A loud crash told him that Shiela had crashed the van on the rocks below. He stopped the car and the two police detectives walked over to the edge of the cliff from which Shiela had plunged about a hundred and fifty feet below into a chasm of boulders.

"She's a goner!" Rogers exclaimed.

"We will have to go down there and check it out," Zeek said, throwing his hands up in a gesture of exasperation.

Slowly they inched their way down the mountain in the new fallen snow that made walking very difficult. Once Zeek fell down and slid about twenty five feet before coming to rest at the foot of a large hemlock tree.

"Here, let me give you a hand," Rogers said pulling him to his feet. "The dame ain't worth the trouble. We should let her freeze and send a crew out in the morning."

"It is just a little bit farther now," Zeek said, walking more briskly as the ground was leveling off. "There it is. Right up there about a hundred feet. We'll make it," he exclaimed.

The van was smashed in the front and in the back. It had hit a large boulder and then had bounced backwards in the snow and come to rest against another boulder that had smashed its rear. The headlights and the taillights had been destroyed in the crash. Utter darkness surrounded them as they peered into the van. The door on the passenger side of the vehicle had been thrown open from the impact.

"I think she is alive," Rogers said as he drew nearer and leaned into the van.

After opening the door on the driver's side, Zeek could see that Shiela was bleeding profusely from her mouth and was pinned down by the column of the steering wheel, but was conscious. On his cell phone, he called for an ambulance. Fortunately the mountain ridge was supplied with cell phone towers and an ambulance was on the way.

"OK, Sister," he said, "help is on the way."

"I don't want your damned help!" Shiela snarled. "You are not going to save me and put me in the gas chamber." Gasping for breath and coughing, Shiela stopped talking and put her hands to her chest. On her face pain was deeply etched, as she continued: "I am glad I poisoned Julian Parnell. The son of a bitch deserved it. He was the only man I ever gave myself to and he was unfaithful and played around with other woman. Just let me die in peace," she begged gasping for breath.

Zeek shone his flash light on Shiela and saw that she was bleeding profusely. When the ambulance arrived and the medics climbed down the hill with a stretcher to remove Shiela from the van, she was dead.

30
Mel

Shiela's admission of guilt set him free from jail and exonerated him from all guilt in the murders that had taken place at Santiago. As soon as he returned to the rectory, he received a phone call from the archbishop.

"Father Mel," he began, "I knew you were not guilty. I want you to come to the chancery tomorrow morning at ten. I need to talk to you about some important issues."

"Of course, Archbishop. I will be there."

The snow had stopped and the sun was shining brightly, when he arrived at the chancery the next morning. Although he was five minutes early, the archbishop's secretary showed him in at once.

Rising to his feet, Hans Fuchs walked around his desk and extending his hand took Mel's hand in his and shook it warmly. "Please be seated. We can sit there at the table by the windows and talk."

Mel sat down and the archbishop took a seat across from him, not at the head of the table, as he might have expected.

"I am sorry for all the grief you have suffered because of the Ardorines. I never should have brought them here. They are leaving tomorrow and will not be back. Their contract ran until next May, but I gave the provincial a cash settlement and got rid of them."

"I heard about how Sister Shiela killed the vicar general and then crashed the van on the mountain roads, but I haven't heard of what happened to Sister Lotta." He waited for the archbishop to explain.

"I was just talking to Hilda, the Mother Provincial, Sister Lotta is in a mental institution, and has completely lost her mind. She thinks she is someone called Abraxas. The prognosis is dismal. Of course, there is always hope." He picked up the carafe of hot coffee that was on the table and poured some into two cups and handed one to Mel.

"Cream and sugar?" he asked.

"Black is fine for me," Mel replied sipping the hot brew.

"I am putting you on a year's sabbatical. You are a good priest and deserve time to recuperate from all you have been through. After the year is up, I will reassign you as pastor at one of our larger parishes."

He could use a year off for spiritual renewal. "But what will happen to Santiago Church?" he asked gazing into Hans Fuch's honest Prussian blue eyes.

"I am closing it down. Actually I have a buyer for it, and the papers for the sale have been signed. You are free to leave at any time."

"I am grateful for the sabbatical, Hans. Thank you for your kindness and for believing in me during this terrible crisis."

Returning to the rectory, he found Monsignor Petit busy packing up his belongings. He had been reassigned to helping out in one of the inner city parishes in downtown Rosanada. He left before nightfall.

Not knowing what he was going to do with his sabbatical, he phoned his parents in New England. When Margaret his mother answered the phone, he greeted her, saying:

"Hi, Mom, I've got a surprise for your and Dad, I am coming home for Christmas. Put another plate on the table. I'll be there about noon on Christmas day."

By the afternoon of Christmas Eve, he was packed and ready to leave, when the door bell rang. Answering the door, he was completely surprised to see Marco Lamadrid standing there smiling at him, "Merry Christmas, Father Mel," Marco greeted him. "May I come in and look around?"

Somewhat puzzled by this request, Mel answered, "Surely, but there is very little to see now. I' m leaving in about an hour. What can I do for you?"

"I am the new owner of Santiago. I bought it from the archdiocese and I am moving in as soon as you leave. Soon it will be Grace Pentecostal Church."

"Merry Christmas, Pastor Marco," Mel said picking up his suitcase and walking out the door, heading for his car.

Immediately Marco began walking from room to room in the rectory saying deliverance prayers to exorcise the evil that had taken possession of Santiago. Tomorrow he would do the same in the rest of the property. He had come home.

It was Christmas Eve and Father Mel stopped in a little country church on the way, as he drove toward New

England and home. When he entered the choir was singing, "O Little Town of Bethlehem." Mel knelt down in the back of the church, as the Mass was just beginning. So much had happened to him. He had been accused of pedophilia and had been sent to Sts. Bachus and Sergius in New Orleans and then had been completely exonerated. Accused of murder, he had been cleared of all charges. The Church was in terrible crisis. Priests and nuns were not faithful to their commitments. Pedophile priests had caused great pain to faithful believers everywhere. Even his former archbishop Cecil L'Abbadon had been an active gay. His present archbishop did not believe the basic doctrines as put forth in the creed. As he knelt in the little country church, he renewed his faith in Jesus Christ. He no longer put his faith in men for they could fail him. Jesus never fails and all his trust was in Him. When the Mass was finished, he rose with faith in his heart and started on his way to New England, singing "Silent night, holy night." The snow had stopped and a bright moon guided his way.

About the Author

Son of an American mother and a Spanish father, Josué Raúl Conte was born in the Principality of Andorra in 1969. After his early education with the Jesuits, he enrolled at Opus Dei University of Navarra in Pamplona, Spain, where he received his doctorate in medieval philosophy and literature. During his years at the university, he became a member of the Neo-catechumenal Way, but later was very disillusioned with the stringent constraints of ultra-conservative Catholicism and adopted a more moderate approach to his faith and left the Way. Having taught at various colleges and universities, he is now a free lance journalist, living in San Francisco with Alicia, his second wife, and Ivan, their Russian wolfhound. Josh Conte is also author of The Stones Cry Out and The Chancery Murders. For more information about him and his works, go to www.listofbestbooks.com.

www.ingramcontent.com/pod-product-compliance
Lightning Source LLC
Chambersburg PA
CBHW020324260626
47156CB00004B/1371

* 9 7 8 1 9 2 6 5 8 5 3 4 5 *